SO CLOSE TO HOME

JAMES BLISH

BALLANTINE BOOKS

NEW YORK

PRINTED IN THE UNITED STATES OF AMERICA

BALLANTINE BOOKS, INC.
101 Fifth Avenue, New York 3, N. Y.

CONTENTS

TO PAT PHILLIPS

STRUGGLE IN THE WOMB

DR. BARNES stood reflectively before the heavy oak door, his hand resting lightly upon the handle. In a way, he was reluctant to go inside and face what was to come; and yet at the same time he was fiercely eager to have it over and done with.

This was the showdown meeting. If it did not evolve into that, Barnes was ready to force it. His left hand carried a brief case full of aces.

A hand touched him lightly on the shoulder. "Dr. Barnes—"

"Eh? Oh, it's you, Ling. What have you found?"

The Chinese technician, only very lately discovered among the long-scattered children of the labor gangs the Japanese had imported, made a curious gesture, as of a woman working a crude loom. "Everywhere. It is as we suspected, Dr. Barnes. I have tapped walls on every floor, and—in each one, I find the web."

"Have you tried cutting it?" Barnes asked.

"Certainly," Han Ling said. "But it will not cut. Anything powerful enough to sever the strands would doubtless destroy the girders of the building as well."

Barnes frowned. Han stood silently, waiting for orders, stroking one lobeless ear absent-mindedly.

"And no current flowing in it? But Ling, that's hardly likely. It can't be putting out all that radiation from nothing. See if the power's being broadcast in. As a last resort, try an Ehrenhaft test."

"Ehrenhaft? But—very well, Dr. Barnes." The young Chinese padded away. Barnes watched him until he disappeared into the polite maw of an elevator. Then with a sudden, decisive gesture, he turned the handle and went in.

It was rather an anticlimax to find the big conference room still deserted. Barnes put his brief case carefully upon the table before his usual seat, made sure the panel cut by Han

Ling in the far wall was closed, and walked over to the window.

It was an interesting vista, if not perhaps an inspiring one. The big white granite office building of the U.N. Atomic Energy Control Commission stood squarely in the center of what had been "old" Nagasaki, almost directly over the spot where the Bomb had fallen so long ago. Barnes could not remember that day, for he had been unborn then; but he was here by a sort of scientific legacy, for his father had been a pile engineer at Hanford.

There was now little trace of the vast bowl of desolation that the Bomb had made. Nagasaki had rebuilt quite rapidly even before the U.N. had become a real world power, but Barnes was still of the opinion that the location of the building was bad psychology. The Japanese did not think in terms of skyscrapers, and this one was an irresistible reminder of that mushroom of destruction that had risen here once. In effect, it froze the smoky column into perdurable stone, a constant reminder.

No wonder that an occasional rattle of gunfire still drifted up to disturb the Mutation Control Board's deliberations.

"Hullo, Barnesy. City-planning again?"

Barnes turned. "Hello, Doull. You might call it that."

Doull thumped his stocky body into a chair and chucked a brown portfolio onto the table with an impatient gesture. "Hope this is quick," he said. "Too damn nice a day to be squabbling over freaks. One thing that Bomb did, Barnesy, it cleaned off the nicest golf course in the whole of Asia."

Barnes returned to his seat, not bothering to conceal his loathing. A moment later Georg Brecht came in with his usual companion, Henry Flecknoe. The two were reported to be engaged in some kind of private physiological research, extraneous to their U.N. studies; Barnes reminded himself to inquire about the project some time.

"The Franciscan not here yet?" Flecknoe said.

"Is he ever on time?" Doull said testily. "The Franciscan" was their usual name for the Board's chairman, Sebastian Xavier Nakamura, D.Sc., F.S.F. In accordance with its usual policy, the U.N. Commission had picked a localite to head local activities; they had dredged Nakamura from a monastery on the edge of the city. Without question the man was a topnotch geneticist, his brilliance reminiscent of that other famous monk-geneticist, Gregor Mendel. But he was an intolerable person, as Barnes meant to establish today.

The door flew open and Nakamura marched across the soft carpet to a nearly audible blare of trumpets. He oozed humility and rectitude. He planted his small frame at the head of the table like a Japanese maple, and said, "Where is Malinov?"

"Sick in quarters," Flecknoe said. "A touch of radiation disease; he has been in the labs too much. He'll be all right."

"Very well," the Franciscan said. "Dr. Doull, you were speaking yesterday of segregating known single-dominant types. Will you proceed, please?"

"Not today," Doull said lazily.

"Dr. Barnes, you are next in order. Have you something to contribute on the subject?"

Barnes looked around the table. If anyone else had urgent business he would be willing to yield. The glances he encountered, however, were merely attentive, except for Brecht's; he had something on his mind, probably something to do with the observation camps, but evidently it wasn't of compelling importance.

"I do," Barnes said. "Segregation I regard as impractical and inhumane; I suggest immediate sterilization of all detected mutants, right down to the double-recessives."

There was a terrible, thunderous silence. Flecknoe slowly turned purple. Doull gaped, apparently convinced that he had lost a word somewhere that would have changed the meaning. Brecht glared. Nakamura blinked politely.

"Eggsplain," Brecht said.

"Gladly. I have evidence to show that the mutation pattern in Nagasaki now shows a majority group; about 40 per cent of the mutants which have been going through our clinics lately have shown the same pattern of physical differences. I will list them for you later."

"Ve are nod empowered," Brecht said, "to eggsercize force against any mutants juzd because he has twelf fingers, or zome udder zuch abnormalidy."

"We are empowered to sterilize if the mutation is dangerous."

"Of course," Flecknoe said. "But we don't get very many mutants who report to us voluntarily, and it's hard to judge by consignments of criminals. What's the point, Barnesy?"

"This, Flecknoe. One: nearly every mutant we have examined in the past eight months has been accused of one of only two crimes: murder, or infanticide. Two: those who killed their own children were for the most part of widely varying types. Three: most of those who committed murder were of the same type."

"And the victims?" the Franciscan said.

"Varying types again. However, the children who were killed *were of the same type as the murderers*."

"I don't get it," Doull complained. "You confuse me, Barnsey. Tell me what you make of all this."

Barnes said, "This mutation type, which I have named *Homo chaos*, is a new, true-breeding, stable species of mankind, quite distinct from *Homo sapiens*. It is now engaged in rubbing out its competition among the more randomized mutations; the murderers are *Homo chaos*, and the citizens of Nagasaki who still belong to *Homo sapiens* or some variant of *Homo sapiens* are, here and there, giving birth to *Homo chaos* babies—and killing them in self-defense!"

Nakamura regarded Barnes with fatherly patience. "Proof?" he said.

"Here." Barnes took a sheaf of papers from his brief case and tossed them to the center of the table. "Complete reports of the examination section. *Homo chaos* looks like any ordinary human on the outside; but inside there are easily recognizable signs. No vermiform appendix; a pineal body that shows up coal-black on the X-rays, even when the pictures are taken through the *foramen magnum;* a type of nervous tissue impervious to silver nitrate; Golgi bodies in the brain do not take silver-line stain. And haemotological signs: very fast clotting time and sedimentation rate; a high white count with a predominance of young forms that you would call mononucleosis in a normal human. And a few other signs."

"That's more than enough for me," Doull declared. "Why bother to have reports typed if you're going to recite 'em aloud anyhow?"

"Bud sterilization?" Brecht said heavily. "Zo eggstreme, Herr Doktor Barnes. Vy? Surely you overeztimade the danger?"

"Do I?" Barnes laughed shortly. "I doubt it. They're foreplanning your children for you right now. I venture to say that any children we have from now on will be *Homo chaos!*"

If Barnes' first demand had caused a sensation, this new assertion was equivalent to the dropping of a Bomb. After a moment Flecknoe got to his feet.

"I move that we ask Dr. Barnes to submit his resignation, effective immediately," he said. "It is obvious that he needs a long rest."

For answer, Barnes strode over to the newly-cut panel in the wall and jerked it open. The golden radiance streamed out; in the aperture, the fine webwork glowed softly.

"That's all through the building," Barnes said. "Our senior engineer, Han Ling, has traced it. It can't be cut, the flow of power in it can't be stopped—and it has nine times the genetic effect of X-rays. God knows how long it's been working on our genes."

He came back to the table, threw another sheaf of papers into the center of it. "Reports of the engineering and radiology sections," he said. "We don't know how the web got there. Dr. Han suspects that it was planted like a seed and grew in the girders. It's my opinion that it isn't matter at all. The radiation acts on exactly nineteen genes, no more. Quite a few of them are on the X-chromosome."

"Shut the damned door, can't you?" Doull said, beginning to fidget.

"What for? It isn't the *light* that's doing the damage, Doull, I assure you. The stuff that's altering your genes—*has* altered them, probably—comes through that panel like light through glass."

There was a long silence.

"Look," Doull said. "So they're dangerous. But if we try to sterilize them all, they'll fight back—and I don't mean just those whistle-strikes they used to stage. Why can't we segregate them? We've got camps."

"And how would you like to be segregated, Doull?"

"That's different; I'm normal."

"Oh," Barnes said silkily. "But that's what they all say, Doull. '*I'm normal—my father had six fingers on each hand, why shouldn't I?*' But as a matter of fact, Doull, you're not normal any more, genetically. You've been sitting in the range of the web. Are you ready to be segregated along with the natives?"

Barnes put his fingertips on the smooth table top. "Gentlemen," he said, "we should have known about this a long time ago. The reason why we did not is that one of our own group has been rerouting much of the important information to the Inactive files—"

Flecknoe began to turn dangerously purple again. "Are you now about to tell us that this radiation makes *somatic* changes, Barnes? We are not idiots—"

He stopped and gaped. It was impossible to see just what had happened. Without the slightest stirring of the air, all the papers in the center of the table had fountained upward, swirling, scattering, as if caught in a sudden tornado. There was no other trace of battle.

Barnes turned green, then gray. He staggered backward, clutching for the arms of his chair. He sat for a while breathing shallowly. His brow was spangled with sweat. Finally he raised his head. Somehow a smile had found its way onto his sick face.

"Proof," he said. "If—I hadn't come—prepared, I'd be dead now. *Homo chaos* is mitogenetic—the Look that Kills, gentlemen. With human beings, it is fatal only to tiny organisms, like yeasts; but *Homo chaos* can kill men. And does."

He struggled to his feet again and swept his papers into his brief case, looking levelly at the man opposite him. "I suggest," he said, "that Frater Nakamura be asked to submit to a medical examination. *He was born here.*"

With that, he reached the door, jerked it open, and then slammed it behind himself.

Inside the room there was dead silence. Then chairs scraped back, slowly, purposefully. Nakamura's voice said, "Gentlemen, if you please—"

"*Swine!*"

"Gentlemen, please—there is another factor—*Homo epipsychos* we have named it—"

Nakamura's voice choked off. Then he screamed. The door shuddered as if something heavy had been thrown against it.

Barnes smiled and turned away. Han Ling was waiting behind him, fingering his lobeless ear reflectively. "Hello, Han. What luck?"

"There's a lead-in cable in the sub-basement, Dr. Barnes. I think we can feed a charge back along it and blow out their power source, wherever it is." He cocked his head toward the door, through which horrid sounds were coming. "But what of Nakamura? Did you kill him?"

"Kill him?" Barnes said. "No. It was only necessary to provoke him into trying mitogenetic murder on me. I suppose they all think I was wearing some sort of shield, but the important thing is that he can't use it on them now. We should be glad that *Homo epipsychos*—"

"*Homo superior*," Han Ling said.

"Well, yes, of course. Still, the name the *Chaos* group has given us is so poetic. In any event, we should be glad we are not so easily detectable as they."

The Chinese abandoned the caressing of his ear and smiled.

"I am pleased," he said. "Had he forced you to kill him personally, we might have been in some danger of betrayal. As it is, we can finish our pogrom without revealing ourselves. I was worried."

"No need to have worried," Barnes said. "I knew I wouldn't have to do the job myself. Human beings are so emotional; tell them somebody's been tampering with their parenthood, and—"

Behind them, Nakamura shrieked. The two mutants disappeared into the polite maw of an elevator.

SPONGE DIVE

I KNOW it sounds funny when I say that Civilian Intelligence Group has traditions to uphold. After all, the outfit isn't very old; it had been going less than ten years when I first began feeling this way about it.

But it's a curious thing about service organizations, whether they're privately owned or run by a government. They can take on this aura of having proud traditions in ten minutes of life—*if* they do something that's of real use to somebody, and that has to be done right or not at all. The Foreign Service, for example; or one of the privately controlled national health foundations.

Contrariwise, a service organization that actually does nobody any good, except its proprietors, can live for a century without developing a tradition with any more meaning than the established time for lunch hour. For example, before coming to CIG I was director of research for what we were told was the oldest advertising agency in the business. The owners *talked* about service and professionalism and loyalty and codes of practice, on the average of one meeting a week; and *still* the turnover there was phenomenal, with two years making you an old-timer. If you stayed there through a third year you were practically a founder; they allowed you to buy stock. This, mind you, for the agency that was rumored to have engineered the Spanish-American War.

I first broached this notion to Joan Hadamard, our titular social sciences division chief—by titular I don't mean that that's not what she is, but that she is actually a great deal more than that—at the beginning of the zirconium affair, and got a healthy snort for my pains. I should have expected it. Joan is an extremely tough-minded, no-nonsense type, about as far from the woolly sociologist as can possibly be imagined, and with all the visible sentiment of a full-grown ocelot.

"I'll settle for balanced books," she said. "That's what it all comes out to in the end. That's why captains go down with their ships; so the owners can prove to the underwriters

14

that the property was occupied when destroyed, and collect the insurance."

"I don't know why I ever listen to you. There's another cherished legend gone up the flue. But Joan, in this case we've got a client to consider, and not any ordinary client either. This thing first came to us from Althor Magnum. The firm's a member of Affiliated Enterprises—one of the very first. I think we ought to make giving them satisfaction the prime aim."

"Not," Joan said, "at the price of going into the red. We don't have to jump for a client just because he belongs to Affiliated Enterprises, Peter. Al Magnum wouldn't put it up to the board if we refused him. He knows he'd be licked."

I accepted this as gospel, because I knew it was. Joan's knowledge of how people and social groups behave emerges from a fundamental difference in her approach. Where other people in her field collect data and construct relations from them, she postulates relations first, derives or predicts behavior from them, and then matches the derivations against the actual actions of people to check them. In other words, she's a disciple of Rashevsky—and she never misses.

Nevertheless, I felt stubborn. I thought I had my reasons. CIG had first come into being because an assorted group of industries and universities—now Affiliated Enterprises, Inc., of which CIG is a wholly owned subsidiary—had wanted to buy an "Ultimac." That is, *the* Ultimac, for no other such computer has ever been built; its limits are unknown, and Clark Cheyney, our mathematics chief (and business manager, incidentally), predicts that we'll never find out what they are. Althor B. Magnum, Inc., one of the country's major industrial research organizations, has been one of those original founders.

It was Magnum himself who brought the problem to us, and it was a nasty one. "Somebody," he said, "is buying all the sponge zirconium on the open market, except for the pure stuff. It's impossible, because every pound of the metal is monitored by the Department of Commerce; it's a critical material. But it's happening. I can't buy any, not even the technical grade, and it's hitting me right where I live. I've got a contract to build a brand new type of research reactor— the design is revolutionary, as I'll show you if you're interested—and all I get from Commerce is, 'So sorry, there's no unallocated zirconium left.' "

I had to confess that I didn't know what the stuff was

good for. Magnum, who began his busniess career as a chemist specializing in organoleptics, knows that nobody knows everything; he didn't mind explaining.

"It's like this, Pete. This stuff used to be scarce, and nothing more than a curiosity. There was only one way of producing it, and that was expensive, and yielded only a few pounds at a time. Then the Bureau of Standards got interested, because it makes a strong structural material, with a melting point way higher than steel, and it has no appetite for neutrons at all; that makes it good for constructing nuclear reactors. So Standards worked out a method for turning it out in big batches, by a modification of the process used to produce sponge titanium. All clear so far?"

I said it was.

"Well, the old method of producing it still has a market, because it yields the pure element, and some people still want that. Usually zirconium occurs in the same ore with hafnium, which is so much like it chemically that they're hell to separate. But for my purposes the Bureau-process product is plenty good enough, and it shouldn't be scarce now. Not any more. I want CIG to find out where it's all going, and cut me a slice."

"Doesn't sound hard," I'd told him. "Of course I can't say right now whether or not we'll take the job. We'll run an assessment on it right away."

"I know," he'd said gloomily. "Sometimes I wonder why I ever sank a dime in this outfit. You've given me three 'noes' in succession this past year."

"It's the budget," I'd explained. "Most of the fund went into Ultimac—you know that. We have to make sure that the fee on a job is commensurate with the costs, or we'll have the trustees on our necks, you included. But I don't think there'll be any trouble on this one. It sounds to me as though the government should be interested; as a matter of fact, they should be raising hell, if they're losing track of anything on the critical list. And their fee on top of yours ought to cover any possible investigation for us very nicely."

With which off-the-cuff opinion, I put my size nine foot in my mouth twice in a single speech. Oh, the government was interested, sure enough. But it turned out that there were *two* possible investigations for us to tackle. One would be cheap and easy, and the government would pay for it, but it wouldn't put a pound of zirconium in Magnum's hands, at least for an indefinite period. The other would unravel the whole affair, get metal to Magnum within the year, would cost ten times what Magnum could afford to pay. And the government wasn't even vaguely interested in that one.

I must confess that I was more than a little appalled when we fed the facts into Ultimac, including the figures which Magnum had supplied us on his proposed research reactor, and got back the twin answers. Zirconium in large quantities, the computer reasoned, is at present useful only for reactors. Anyone buying the metal in the limited quantities available on the open market, as opposed to someone being allocated relatively unlimited amounts by his government, could be building (a) one or two huge reactors, or (b) a flock of small ones. The huge reactors predicated would be highly inefficient for any possible job a reactor might be called upon to do, at the present state of the art. *Ergo,* small reactors were involved.

Small reactors are bombs.

Q.E.D.

So, somebody was buying U.S. zirconium to make atom bombs. By the time I got this far into the protocol the computer had handed me, I was feeling pretty complacent about the chances that the government would pay us a fat fee for Magnum's project.

"It is unlikely that the purchasers of the metal are building these weapons inside the continental United States, the probability being below the significant level by the chi-square test," the protocol went on. (Ultimac's style isn't set for drama; only for content.) "The immediate buyer(s) in the United States, therefore, ship(s) the material elsewhere. This phase of the operation could be terminated by finding out what operations in the government itself make the buying possible.

"After this problem is solved, the significant probabilities are that the purchased material is leaving the country disguised as sponge platinum, which it resembles and which is a normal item of commerce, regularly exported by the U.S. The market for sponge platinum may be classified into two categories: (1) the chemical catalyst market, and (2) the jewelry market. Category 1 involves the largest potential area of search, embracing all industrialized countries; but it may be effectively ruled out of the problem, since in this category platinum itself is a subcritical material and its shipment is already policed by the government. In category 2, the two high probabilities are the Netherlands and the Scandinavian

Peninsula, with the latter again of lower probability, since it also falls in category 1. Thus recovery of the material is most likely to be obtained through the Dutch jewelry bourse."

And there it was. We then proposed to the government, not with much hope, that it pay for a fishing expedition abroad. We got a flat No. All the government wanted us to do was to shut off the pipeline; it wasn't interested in recovering unallocated metal. It was at this point that I tried to make my point about CIG tradition, with the resounding success reported above.

But, also as reported, I was stubborn. I knew better than to try to maneuver Joan into anything. She knows all the mechanisms ever invented for doing that, and two more besides. My only chance was to come up with something that had genuine validity in her eyes *and* in the eyes of the machine.

Naturally I started with the machine, in the hope of getting more data. The data I got made me feel the ship going down around me with even greater celerity than before. It appeared that what Ultimac had meant by "the Dutch jewelry bourse" wasn't in Amsterdam, but in two other places entirely. For various reasons, chiefly Holland's past fate in various European wars and her likeliest fate if another war broke out in the future, the Dutch gemstone and jewelry craftsmen and traders had relocated in large numbers in São Paulo, where gems are as common as perfume in Paris. A still greater number had gone to South Africa, right to the edges of the mines, so to speak. So the search became a matter of going to Amsterdam and finding who was receiving the zirconium there, then following it to wherever they were shipping it. It would be incredibly expensive.

Then we got the money.

"I don't think I understand this," I told Clark Cheyney. "You mean we've been forbidden to undertake the big job, but given the money for it? Or, contrariwise, that we've been authorized to do the little job, and given a hundredfold too large an appropriation for it?"

"Both," Cheyney said in his slow bank-president's voice. "It's obviously a clerical error. Some clerk processing our two proposals has attached the estimates of each one to the protocols of the other. Now that the small search has been okayed, the big checks are coming in, regular as clockwork."

"Well, what are we going to do? Got any ideas, Joan? Shall we undertake the big job, now that the money is here?"

"We don't dare," Joan said. "Sooner or later the accounting department up at Commerce is going to discover the mistake. Bear in mind that Commerce isn't authorized to issue a nickel for any foreign operation. At that point, the checks will begin to bounce."

"And whoever's doing the job would be stranded," I agreed glumly. "Well, we can always go ahead and do what we've been authorized to do, and return the rest of the money."

"Wasteful," Clark said gravely. "If there is more money available than what we need, more will be spent. That's inevitable."

"If we keep a close eye on it—"

"More'll be spent anyhow," Joan said. "Even with the tightest bookkeeping, the mere knowledge that the extra money is there will create unconscious waste. Slightly more expensive accommodations, slightly longer cab rides, a little more equipment than is actually needed to produce a given piece of information . . . it mounts up. And our field operatives have never been trained to pinch pennies. Sure, they don't pad their expense accounts—at least not beyond expectation— but they're never supposed to be niggardly. It won't do."

"We'll be asked to account for the overage when the mistake is discovered," Cheyney added. "The only proper thing to do is to turn the money back promptly, and resubmit the proposals. Stapled together, I would suggest."

"And do nothing in the meantime?" I said. "Where would that leave Magnum?"

"Nowhere," Joan said. "But Clark's right; it's the only course."

I stood up. "That may well be," I said grimly. "You go ahead and start the red tape unwinding. But somewhere in the world somebody is making bombs out of that zirconium, and we don't know what they plan to do with them. Over here, one of our own founders can't fulfill an obligation for want of the stuff—which means because of our inaction. I won't sit still for it. It isn't right."

"What are you going to do?" Cheyney said.

"He's going overseas himself," Joan said. "What are you going to use for money, Peter?"

"I'm going to draw on the general fund," I said. "And keep drawing on it, until either the problem is solved, or CIG is broke. If you don't want to see CIG broke, Clark, you'd better think up a fourth solution to this financial hassle. But I think this means more to us than money."

Cheyney said nothing, since I was authorized to draw on the general fund and he knew it. But there was actual pain in his eyes.

Johannesburg. I was sitting in a rickety black café in the worst slum in South Africa when Roger Balim finally brought me my man. There was a wind-up phonograph on the bar playing American jazz of a vintage two or three years in the bottle. The Negro diamond miners, filthy and clean, glum and gay, squatted on the floor drinking palm wine; there were very few tables. I had one, but that was only because I had with me the foreman of Pit Six and two other black men of standing in the community. Even so, nobody looked at me with anything but a brooding, resigned suspicion. And not only at me; they looked at my companions that way, too, as though they knew they would never know who would turn his coat next.

Some of the miners were dancing, American style, but without any discrimination as to sex; some of the dancing couples were mixed, some were not. They danced to dance, not as a form of courting. A few danced alone, and one grimy old man had found an open space in which to do a tribal figure he alone remembered, all by himself. He moved his hands as though he were shaking gourds, though his hands were empty, and his feet stamped out the ancient measures of war or love or medicine . . . All to the tune of "I've Got a Rocket in the Locket in My Pocket (to se-e-end my heart to you)."

The smoke was terrific. The flies didn't seem to mind.

Balim had been my stroke of luck for this leg of the journey: a real, 24-carat heel, the kind of guy from whom you can buy anything, up to and including his grandmother. Of course, he had been a little nervous about it, but in the end money won. With him it always would.

Out of moderate pity for CIG's general fund, I had played my hunch right out to the end and gone directly to Johannesburg. My reasoning was fairly airtight by my standards, though I'd have hated to know then what Ultimac thought of it.

Zirconium may be useful in bombs but it isn't the ingredient that makes the bomb go bang. For that you need fissionables. Brazil has a government atomic industry of its own, capable of producing plutonium in quantity; nobody was going to be shipping that much coal to São Paulo. South Africa, on the other hand, was still behind most large nations in the nuclear field; but it has gold, and where there is gold there is always uranium, usually cheek by jowl. Furthermore, despite Apartheid and some even more barbarous customs, the Union is just as industrialized as Brazil, and has just as much bush where anything, of any size, might be hidden. Somebody there could well be building bombs in secret.

Somebody was. It was easy to find that out, once I was reasonably sure what I was looking for. I found it in the Johannesburg phone book. The Delft Company, Jewelry Brokers. A dead giveaway, for nobody deals in diamonds in Africa but de Beers; nobody sets any jewel but diamonds; and the legitimate cutters, setters, and traders, Dutch though most of them are in staff and ownership, do not take Dutch names. The Union is too intensely nationalistic to make such names good business.

A little prying, a little pressure, a little money, and I knew Roger Balim was my man. He was a native Afrikander, white, university-educated, highly skilled in some very recondite branches of engineering which couldn't have anything to do with lapidary work *or* jewelry brokerage. He was one of a number of such men on Delft's staff, but the rest were so closemouthed that I didn't dare even approach them. Balim was different; I had only to tell him that I knew the "platinum" the firm was signing for from Holland wasn't platinum at all, and he was asking me how much I'd take to keep my mouth shut.

Somebody changed the record on the phonograph. Now it was something pseudo-Hawaiian, complete with seasick steel-guitar glissandi. The old man looked discombobulated and sat down cross-legged on the floor, where he began to rock with steady, hypnotic dignity. There was a cadaverous dog being sick right next to him, but he didn't seem to notice.

I had asked Balim how much *he* would take to tell me where the zirconium was being routed out of Johannesburg. He was glad enough to find out that I wanted to bribe, rather than be bribed, but he was scared. He wouldn't tell me directly, but for a price he offered to introduce me to a man who *might* tell me.

There they came across the floor now, Balim looking apprehensively for me. Sure enough, there was another man with him. He was a real shock.

He was a thin Negro, well over six feet tall, clad in a loose white duck suit, a white shirt, open at the collar, from which wrists and neck emerged as gaunt as those of a corpse. Though his clothes must have been broilingly hot, he gave not the slightest sign of discomfort; nor did he take any notice of the din, or of the looks that were given him as he followed Balim.

They were peculiar, those looks. Forgive me, but Christ dragging the cross to Calvary must have been looked at like that by the poor in the crowd. And there was indeed something very messiah-like about his expression: fierce as a condor, yet withdrawn, suffering, patient, distant. He had high cheekbones whch stood out cruelly against his taut skin, and his eyes glittered. I don't remember ever seeing him blink, though of course he must have; everyone's eyeballs have to be lubricated sometimes, or sight goes. I don't think he was a Bantu; the notion crossed my mind that he must have come from one of the nomad tribes that roam the deserts of the borders of Upper Kenya, but perhaps I was only being reminded of John the Baptist.

"Here's the man I was telling you about," Balim said to me, with an odd gesture. I think he was trying to warn me to be circumspect. If so, he was going to get a nasty shock. "This is Piara Singh. This is Mr. Bellows, from America."

Singh sat down directly, and lifted his hand to each of my three companions. Had I not known that Singh was coming, I could never have had them with me at all, and hence could never have gotten into the café; Balim had arranged that, too. They rose ceremonially, but Singh gestured them down again.

"You wanted to see me, Mr. Bellows," he said in excellent English, looking at me with those gleaming, intense eyes.

"Yes. I'm very grateful to you for coming. But my name is not Bellows; it's Harris, Dr. Peter Harris. Mr. Bellows was only a convenience."

"You are honest," Singh said, staring at me from under the prominent ridges of his eyebrows. And I believed him; I knew that somebody had looked right into me, and what he had said thereafter was a statement of fact. "Piara Singh is also a convenience. It is as common a Hindu name as John Smith is an American name; its truth is only that my faith is Hindu. But I cannot be honest with you further, for I must maintain the fiction."

"This is honorable," I said. I was treading very lightly. I had only an inkling of what I was dealing with, but I knew that with this man nothing would do but the ultimate courtesy of believing every word he said. "I'm here because I think I can do you a service, and do myself a service too. You are buying metal from Mr. Balim here. I know why you want it. You are probably paying too much for it."

"Now, wait a minute," Balim said, flushing.

Singh said, "I know that. We can get it no other way. This is not the service Dr. Harris wishes to do me, Roger."

He frightened me; he saw things. "No, it isn't," I said. "I'm only sorry that it has to be so. But the service is this: you will not win what you want with these weapons you are building."

"Ah," Singh said. He looked at me quite a long time. Then he said, "That also is true. But I do not see why. Please explain it to me."

"Wait a minute," Balim said again. "Harris, what's the reason for the phony name? What kind of game are you playing? I thought you wanted the metal yourself, and would pay for it. You'd damn well better not mix into something you don't understand."

"I'm from Civilian Intelligence Group, Balim," I told him. "We have a reputation. Are you sure you understand what that means, or hadn't you better shut up?"

Balim did more than shut up. He got up, his face white. Singh reached out a clawlike, sinewy hand and pulled him down again without the slightest show of effort, although I would guess that he weighed thirty pounds less than Balim.

"Please explain," he said.

"Gladly. But first, please tell me what your plans are for the bombs. Otherwise I shan't understand the affair well enough to explain it."

"We will drop a few in Johannesburg," Singh said. "For the effect. It has been planned for a long time, but we did not expect to be able to use these new bombs; that was lucky for us, getting them. If a few do not serve, we will drop more, all on the government buildings, until the government will abandon the Apartheid policy."

His fingertip touched my knuckles. It was as though a live wire had dropped there.

"That is the beginning," he said. "We are thousands and thousands strong. We have sworn that we will have our own country back. We have sworn both the earth oath and the blood oath. We have white men like Mr. Balim to help us with technical matters; we pay them in gold, so we can be sure of them. They have shown us how to build the plant and make the weapons. We have our own pilots. To get the fuel

—and the gold—has cost us many lives already, but we have hordes who will die when we ask them to. Better to die that way, than to die of silicosis, or TB, or kicked to death in the middle of a city street by a policeman. Is that not so?"

"I can't say, because I don't know," I said. "But I know this: these bombs are not what you think they are. Only one of them, even if you drop it only on a government building, will destroy Johannesburg all the way out to here, and beyond. Death for the whole city—and for everything you plan."

Slowly, Singh turned and looked at Balim. I hope no man ever looks at me like that. Balim looked down at the ground.

Evidently Singh did not need to ask him any question, let alone hear any answer. He said to me: "We were not told. We do not seek massacre; that error has already been made. Nor do we want our own people to die at our own hands."

"I know. That's why I tell you what I do."

He was silent a long while. Then he said, "Tell me what we should do."

I had thought about that as intensively as I could, and nothing that had occurred to me was easy. All I can say for my advice is that it was the best I had to offer. That's not saying very much.

"Give it up," I said. They were the hardest three words I ever spoke in my life. "Violence isn't the way. As a Hindu, you know that in your heart. A wise man in the West said, 'After the first death, there is no other.' The little bomb and the big bombs you're making are alike. They kill. The numbers of dead don't matter. One is too many. Do it the hard way."

"Everything you say is true," Singh said. He was staring at the murky air far over my head. His voice was that of a man who has just been condemned, and somehow feels his heart breaking with gladness to hear the sentence. I could hardly bear it. "Perhaps I have known it. But the word needed to be spoken."

"I can help a little," I said. I had a frog in my throat. "I'll see to it that Balim's company buys back the zirconium at exactly the price you paid for it. The company will then give it to me, for nothing, because the United States will ask it to, quietly but emphatically. You'll do that, won't you, Roger?"

Balim was sweating dirt. He nodded without looking up.

"I can't dispose of your assembled bombs," I said. "But I can probably negotiate some sort of contract for your refined uranium isotope. My superiors will be interested in anything that will break the virtual monopoly they have up north in the Congo. I know this doesn't begin to cover your losses, but perhaps that's not the major question. If you offer to sell your refining plant to your government at cost, you'll have an explosion worth producing. The story—an all-African atomic power industry created privately, from sheer guts—will go all around the world. Isn't that worth while?"

Singh nodded, his eyes still remote, and waited.

"That's all," I said. "I'm sorry. I realize that it isn't very much. But it's all I have to offer."

Singh's eyes came down to me, as though with great effort. For a moment I saw nothing in the world but those tortured black pools. Then his strangely high voice said:

"It is a great gift. You are our brother, Dr. Harris. We have a saying: 'Only the wise have love in their blood.' May it always be so."

And he was gone, and poor dollar-damned Balim with him. I swear that I never saw them go, but suddenly there was no one with me but the three men from Pit Six. They shook hands with me and we had palm wine all around.

Shipping that zirconium home was going to take CIG's general fund down to minus nothing, but I didn't care. Somebody had put another record on the phonograph. It was "I'd Push a Tank Clear Up Mount Blanc (just for the love of you)." The old man got up and began to pound out his solitary triumph, barefoot, dirty, lonely, and unconquerable. I wanted to dance, myself.

"Singh is an educated man," I told Joan and Cheyney. "But his education has holes in it, and he can't wipe out his tribal childhood. When I got to the plant, I found that every one of those bombs had a witch-mark on it, smeared on in goat's dung. There was a special compound for the goats, right in the plant. and they had a spot on the assembly line where the dung was put on. And another compound where they kept black roosters, to supply blood to sprinkle the bombs with just before they were loaded into those old surplus planes."

"The turncoats," Joan said, "were going to let them saturate Johannesburg with the bombs; all the planes would have been lost in the process. Then they were going to betray Singh, and the location of the plant. In the universal horror, people like Balim would get quietly away wth the money Singh had paid them."

"It looks that way," I said. "Speaking of money, what do we do now? I did for the general fund, but good. I only got back by flashing my ID card so I could get tickets on the cuff."

"Oh, that," Cheyney said. "What you did for our standing is much more important, Peter. Especially since the general fund is intact."

"Intact? Impossible—I must have spent—"

"It's quite intact," Cheyney said. "You put us on the spot, Peter. Just as you said at the time, we *had* to think up a fourth way out. There was only one other way, and Joan used it."

"What on earth was it?"

"I took it straight to the White House," Joan said composedly. "And I scared the old man green."

After I had taken it in, I saw the amusement in her cool gray eyes. I began to laugh myself.

"*Brother,*" I said. "I'll bet you did."

ONE-SHOT

ON THE DAY that the Polish freighter *Ludmilla* laid an egg in New York harbor, Abner Longmans ("One-Shot") Braun was in the city going about his normal business, which was making another million dollars. As we found out later, almost nothing else was normal that particular weekend for Braun. For one thing, he had brought his family with him—a complete departure from routine—reflecting the unprecedentedly legitimate nature of the deals he was trying to make. From every point of view it was a bad weekend for the CIG to mix into his affairs, but nobody had explained that to the master of the *Ludmilla*.

I had better add here that we knew nothing about this until afterward. From the point of view of the storyteller, an organization like Civilian Intelligence Group gets to all its facts backwards, entering the tale at the pay-off, working back to the hook, and winding up with a sheaf of background facts to feed into the computer for Next Time. It's rough on various people who've tried to fictionalize what we do—particularly the lazy examples of the breed, who come to us expecting to find their plotting already done for them—but it's inherent in the way we operate, and there it is.

Certainly nobody at CIG so much as thought of Braun when the news first came through. Harry Anderton, the Harbor Defense chief, called us at 0830 Friday to take on the job of identifying the egg; this is when our records show us officially entering the affair. But of course Anderton had been keeping the wires to Washington steaming for an hour before that, getting authorization to spend some of his money on us (our clearance status was then and is now C&R—clean and routine).

I was in the central office when the call came through, and had some difficulty in making out precisely what Anderton wanted of us. "Slow down, Colonel Anderton, please," I begged him. "Two or three seconds won't make that much

27

difference. How did you find out about this egg in the first place?"

"The automatic compartment bulkheads on the *Ludmilla* were defective," he said. "It seems that this egg was buried among a lot of other crates in the dump-cell of the hold—"

"What's a dump-cell?"

"It's a sea lock for getting rid of dangerous cargo. The bottom of it opens right to Davy Jones. Standard fitting for ships carrying explosives, radioactives, anything that might act up unexpectedly."

"All right," I said. "Go ahead."

"Well, there was a timer on the dump-cell floor, set to drop the egg when the ship came up the river. That worked fine, but the automatic bulkheads that are supposed to keep the rest of the ship from being flooded while the cell's open, didn't. At least they didn't do a thorough job. The *Ludmilla* began to list and the captain yelled for help. When the Harbor Patrol found the dump-cell open, they called us in."

"I see." I thought about it a moment. "In other words, you don't know whether the *Ludmilla* really laid an egg or not."

"That's what I keep trying to explain to you, Dr. Harris. We don't know what she dropped and we haven't any way of finding out. It could be a bomb, it could be anything. We're sweating everybody on board the ship now, but it's my guess that none of them know anything; the whole procedure was designed to be automatic."

"All right, we'll take it," I said. "You've got divers down?"

"Sure, but—"

"We'll worry about the buts from here on. Get us a direct line from your barge to the big board here so we can direct the work. Better get on over here yourself."

"Right." He sounded relieved. Official people have a lot of confidence in CIG—too much, in my estimation. Some day the job will come along that we can't handle, and then Washington will be kicking itself—or, more likely, some scapegoat—for having failed to develop a comparable government department.

Not that there was much prospect of Washington's doing that. Official thinking had been running in the other direction for years. The precedent was the Associated Universities organization which ran Brookhaven; CIG had been started the same way, by a loose corporation of universities and industries, all of which had wanted to own an Ultimac and no one of which had the money to buy one for itself. The

Eisenhower administration, with its emphasis on private enterprise and concomitant reluctance to sink federal funds into projects of such size, had turned the two examples into a nice fat trend, which Ultimac herself said wasn't going to be reversed within the practicable lifetime of CIG.

I buzzed for two staffers, and in five minutes got Clark Cheyney and Joan Hadamard, CIG's business manager and social science division chief respectively. The titles were almost solely for the benefit of the T/O. That is, Clark and Joan do serve in those capacities, but said service takes about two per cent of their capacities and their time. I shot them a couple of sentences of explanation, trusting them to pick up whatever else they needed from the tape, and checked the line to the divers' barge.

It was already open; Anderton had gone to work quickly and with decision once he was sure we were taking on the major question. The television screen lit up, but nothing showed on it but murky light, striped with streamers of darkness slowly rising and falling. The audio went *cloonck . . . oing, oing . . . bonk . . . oing . . .* Underwater noises, shapeless and characterless.

"Hello, out there in the harbor. This is CIGA, Harris calling. Come in, please."

"Monig here," the audio said. *Boink . . . oing, oing . . .*

"Got anything yet?"

"Not a thing, Dr. Harris," Monig said. "You can't see three inches in front of your face down here—it's too silty. We've bumped into a couple of crates, but so far, no egg."

"Keep trying."

Cheyney, looking even more like a bulldog than usual, was setting his stopwatch by one of the eight clocks on Ultimac's face. "Want me to take the divers?" he said.

"No, Clark, not yet. I'd rather have Joan do it for the moment." I passed the mike to her. "You'd better run a probability series first."

"Check." He began feeding tape into the integrator's mouth. "What's your angle, Peter?"

"The ship. I want to see how heavily shielded that dump-cell is."

"It isn't shielded at all," Anderton's voice said behind me. I hadn't heard him come in. "But that doesn't prove anything. The egg might have carried sufficient shielding on itself. Or maybe the Commies didn't care whether the crew was exposed or not. Or maybe there isn't any egg."

"All that's possible," I admitted. "But I want to see it, anyhow."

"Have you taken blood tests?" Joan asked Anderton.

"Yes."

"Get the reports through to me, then. I want white-cell counts, differentials, platelet counts, hematocrit and sed rates on every man."

Anderton picked up the phone and I took a firm hold on the doorknob.

"Hey," Anderton said, putting the phone down again. "Are you going to duck out just like that? Remember, Dr. Harris, we've got to evacuate the city first of all! No matter whether it's a real egg or not—we can't take the chance on it's *not* being an egg!"

"Don't move a man until you get a go-ahead from CIG," I said. "For all we know now, evacuating the city may be just what the enemy wants us to do—so they can grab it unharmed. Or they may want to start a panic for some reason, any one of fifty possible reasons."

"You can't take such a gamble," he said grimly. "There are eight and a half million lives riding on it. I can't let you do it."

"You passed your authority to us when you hired us," I pointed out. "If you want to evacuate without our O.K., you'll have to fire us first. It'll take another hour to get that cleared from Washington, so you might as well give us the hour."

He stared at me for a moment, his lips thinned. Then he picked up the phone again to order Joan's blood count, and I got out the door, fast.

A reasonable man would have said that I found nothing useful on the *Ludmilla,* except negative information. But the fact is that anything I found would have been a surprise to me. I went down looking for surprises. I found nothing but a faint trail to Abner Longmans Braun, most of which was fifteen years cold.

There'd been a time when I'd known Braun, briefly and with no profit to either of us. As an undergraduate majoring in social sciences, I'd taken on a term paper on the old International Longshoreman's Association, a racket-ridden union now formally extinct, although anyone who knew the signs could still pick up some traces on the docks. In those days, Braun had been the business manager of an insurance firm, the sole visible function of which had been to write policies for the ILA and its individual dockwallopers. For some reason, he had been amused by the brash youngster who'd barged in on him and demanded the low-down, and had shown me considerable lengths of ropes not normally in view of the public—nothing incriminating, but enough to give me a better insight into how the union operated than I had had any right to expect—or even suspect.

Hence I was surprised to hear somebody on the docks remark that Braun was in the city over the weekend. It would never have occurred to me that he still interested himself in the waterfront, for he'd gone respectable with a vengeance. He was still a professional gambler, and according to what he had told the Congressional Investigating Committee last year, took in thirty to fifty thousand dollars a year at it, but his gambles were no longer concentrated on horses, the numbers, or shady insurance deals. Nowadays what he did was called investment—mostly in real estate; realtors knew him well as a man who had *almost* bought the Empire State Building. (The *almost* in the equation stands for the moment when the shoestring broke.)

Joan had been following his career, too, not because she had ever met him, but because for her he was a type study in the evolution of what she called "the extralegal ego." "With personalities like that, respectability is a disease," she told me. "There's always an almost open conflict between the desire to be powerful and the desire to be accepted; your ordinary criminal is a moral imbecile, but people like Braun are damned with a conscience, and sooner or later they crack trying to appease it."

"I'd sooner try to crack a Timken bearing," I said. "Braun's ten-point steel all the way through."

"Don't you believe it. The symptoms are showing all over him. Now he's backing Broadway plays, sponsoring beginning actresses, joining playwrights' groups—he's the only member of Buskin and Brush who's never written a play, acted in one, or so much as pulled the rope to raise the curtain."

"That's investment," I said. "That's his business."

"Peter, you're only looking at the surface. His real investments almost never fail. But the plays he backs *always* do. They have to; he's sinking money in them to appease his conscience, and if they were to succeed it would double his guilt instead of salving it. It's the same way with the young actresses. He's not sexually interested in them—his type never is, because living a rigidly orthodox family life is part of the effort toward respectability. He's backing them to pay his debts to society—in other words, they're talismans to keep him out of jail."

"It doesn't seem like a very satisfactory substitute."

"Of course it isn't," Joan had said. "The next thing he'll do is go in for direct public service—giving money to hospitals or something like that. You watch."

She had been right. Within a year, Braun had announced the founding of an association for clearing the Detroit slum area where he had been born—the plainest kind of symbolic suicide: *Let's not have any more Abner Longmans Brauns born down here*. It depressed me to see it happen, for next on Joan's agenda for Braun was an entry into politics as a fighting liberal, a New Dealer twenty years too late. Since I'm mildly liberal myself when I'm off duty, I hated to think what Braun's career might tell me about my own motives, if I'd let it.

All of which had nothing to do with why I was prowling around the *Ludmilla*. Or did it? I kept remembering Anderton's challenge: "You can't take such a gamble. There are eight and a half million lives riding on it—" That put it up into Braun's normal operating area all right. The connection was still hazy, but on the grounds that any link might be useful I phoned him.

He remembered me instantly. Like most uneducated, power-driven men, he had a memory as good as any machine's.

"You never did send me that paper you was going to write," he said. His voice seemed absolutely unchanged, although he was now in his seventies. "You promised you would."

"Kids don't keep their promises as well as they should," I said. "But I've still got copies and I'll see to it that you get one this time. Right now I need another favor—something right up your alley."

"CIG business?"

"Yes. I didn't know you knew I was with CIG."

Braun chuckled. "I still know a thing or two," he said. "What's the angle?"

"That I can't tell you over the phone. But it's the biggest gamble there ever was, and I think we need an expert. Can you come down to CIG's central headquarters right away?"

"Yeah, if it's that big. If it ain't, I got lots of business here, Pete. And I ain't going to be in town long. You're sure it's top stuff?"

"My word on it."

He was silent a moment. Then he said, "Pete, send me your paper."

"The paper? Sure, but—" Then I got it. I'd given him my word. "You'll get it," I said. "Thanks, Mr. Braun."

I called headquarters and sent a messenger to my apartment to look for one of those old, dusty blue folders with the legal-length sheets inside them, with orders to scorch it over to Braun without stopping to breathe more than once. Then I went back myself.

The atmosphere had changed. Anderton was sitting by the big desk, clenching his fists and sweating; his whole posture telegraphed controlled helplessness. Cheyney was bent over a seismograph, echo-sounding for the egg through the river bottom. If that had even a prayer of working, I knew, he'd have had the trains of the Hudson & Manhattan stopped; their rumbling course through their tubes would have blanked out any possible echo-pip from the egg.

"Wild goose chase?" Joan said, scanning my face.

"Not quite. I've got something, if I can just figure out what it is. Remember One-Shot Braun?"

"Yes. What's he got to do with it?"

"Nothing," I said. "But I want to bring him in. I don't think we'll lick this project before deadline without him."

"What good is a professional gambler on a job like this? He'll just get in the way."

I looked toward the television screen which now showed an amorphous black mass jutting up from a foundation of even deeper black. "Is that operation getting you anywhere?"

"Nothing's gotten us anywhere," Anderton interjected harshly. "We don't even know if that's the egg—the whole area is littered with crates. Harris, you've got to let me get that alert out!"

"Clark, how's the time going?"

Cheyney consulted the stopwatch. "Deadline in twenty-nine minutes," he said.

"All right, let's use those minutes. I'm beginning to see this thing a little clearer. Joan, what we've got here is a one-shot gamble; right?"

"In effect," she said cautiously.

"And it's my guess that we're never going to get the answer by diving for it—not in time, anyhow. Remember when the

Navy lost a bargeload of shells in the harbor, back in '52?
They scrabbled for them for a year and never pulled up a
one; they finally had to warn the public that if it found anything funnylooking along the shore it shouldn't bang said
object, or shake it either. We're better equipped than the
Navy was then, but we're working against a deadline."

"If you'd admitted that earlier," Anderton said hoarsely,
"we'd have half a million people out of the city by now.
Maybe even a million."

"We haven't given up yet, Colonel. The point is this, Joan:
what we need is an inspired guess. Get anything from the
prob series, Clark? I thought not. On a one-shot gamble of
this kind, the 'laws' of chance are no good at all. For that
matter, the so-called ESP experiments showed us long ago
that even the way we construct random tables is full of holes,
and that a man with a feeling for the essence of a gamble
can make a monkey out of chance almost at will.

"And if there ever was such a man, Braun is it. That's
why I asked him to come down here. I want him to look at
that lump on the screen and—play a hunch."

"You're out of your mind," Anderton said.

A decorous knock spared me the trouble of having to
deny, affirm, or ignore the judgment. It was Braun; the messenger had been fast, and the gambler hadn't bothered to
read what a college student had thought of him fifteen years
ago. He came forward and held out his hand, while the
others looked him over frankly.

He was impressive all right. It would have been hard for
a stranger to believe that he was aiming at responsibility;
to the eye, he was already there. He was tall and spare and
walked perfectly erect, not without spring despite his age.
His clothing was as far from that of a gambler as you could
have taken it by design; a black double-breasted suit with a
thin vertical stripe, a gray silk tie with a pearl stickpin just
barely large enough to be visible at all, a black Homburg;
all perfectly fitted, all worn wth proper casualness—one
might almost say a formal casualness. It was only when he
opened his mouth that One-Shot Braun was in the suit with
him.

"I come over as soon as your runner got to me," he said.
"What's the pitch, Pete?"

"Mr. Braun, this is Joan Hadamard, Clark Cheyney, Colonel Anderton. I'll be quick because we need speed now. A
Polish ship has dropped something out in the harbor. We

don't know what it is. It may be a hell-bomb, or it may be just somebody's old laundry. Obviously we've got to find out which—and we want you to tell us."

Braun's aristocratic eyebrows went up. "Me? Hell, Pete, I don't know nothing about things like that. I'm surprised with you. I thought CIG had all the brains it needed. Ain't you got machines to tell you answers like that?"

I pointed silently to Joan, who had gone back to work the moment the introductions were over. She was still on the mike to the divers. She was saying: "What does it look like?"

"It's just a lump of something, Dr. Hadamard. Can't even tell its shape, it's buried too deeply in the mud." *Cloonk . . . Oing, oing . . .*

"Try the Geiger."

"We did. Nothing but background."

"Scintillation counter?"

"Nothing, Dr. Hadamard. Could be it's shielded."

"Let us do the guessing, Monig. All right, maybe it's got a clockwork fuse that didn't break with the impact. Or a gyroscopic fuse. Stick a stethoscope on it and see if you pick up a ticking or anything that sounds like a motor running."

There was a lag and I turned back to Braun. "As you can see, we're stymied. This is a long shot, Mr. Braun. One throw of the dice—one showdown hand. We've got to have an expert call it for us, somebody with a record of hits on long shots. That's why I called you."

"It's no good," He took off the Homburg, took his handkerchief from his breast pocket, and wiped the hatband. "I can't do it."

"Why not?"

"It ain't my *kind* of thing," he said. "Look, I never in my life run odds on anything that made any difference. But this makes a difference. If I guess wrong—"

"Then we're all dead ducks. But why should you guess wrong? Your hunches have been working for sixty years now."

Braun wiped his face. "No. You don't get it. I wish you'd listen to me. Look, my wife and kids are in the city. It ain't only my life, it's theirs, too. That's what I care about. That's why it's no good. On things that matter to me, *my hunches don't work.*"

I was stunned, and so, I could see, were Joan and Cheyney.

I suppose I should have guessed it, but it had never occurred to me.

"Ten minutes," Cheyney said.

I looked up at Braun. He was frightened, and again I was surprised without having any right to be. I tried to keep my voice calm.

"Please try anyhow, Mr. Braun—as a favor. It's already too late to do it any other way. And if you guess wrong, the outcome won't be any worse than if you don't try at all."

"My kids," he whispered. I don't suppose he knew he was speaking aloud. I waited.

Then his eyes seemed to come back to the present. "All right," he said. "I told you the truth, Pete. Remember that. So—is it a bomb or ain't it? That's what's up for grabs, right?"

I nodded. He closed his eyes. An unexpected stab of pure fright went down my back. Without the eyes, Braun's face was a death mask.

The water sounds and the irregular ticking of a Geiger counter seemed to spring out from the audio speaker four times as loud as before. I could even hear the pen of the seismograph scribbling away until I looked at the instrument and saw that Clark had stopped it, probably long ago.

Droplets of sweat began to form along Braun's forehead and his upper lip. The handkerchief remained crushed in his hand.

Anderton said, "Of all the fool—"

"Hush!" Joan said quietly.

Slowly, Braun opened his eyes. "All right," he said. "You guys wanted it this way. *I say it's a bomb.*" He stared at us for a moment more. And then, all at once, the Timken bearing burst. Words poured out of it. "Now you guys do something, do your job like I did mine. Get my wife out of there. Empty the city. Do something, do *something!*"

Anderton was already grabbing for the phone. "You're right, Mr. Braun. If it isn't already too late—"

Cheyney shot out a hand and caught Anderton's telephone arm by the wrist. "Wait a minute," he said.

"What d'you mean, 'wait a minute'? Haven't you already shot enough time?"

Cheyney did not let go. Instead, he looked inquiringly at Joan and said, "One minute, Joan. You might as well go ahead."

She nodded and spoke into the mike. "Monig, unscrew the cap."

"Unscrew the cap?" the audio squawked. "But Dr. Hadamard, if that sets it off—"

"It won't go off. That's the one thing you can be sure it won't do."

"What is this?" Anderton demanded. "And what's this deadline stuff, anyhow?"

"The cap's off," Monig reported. "We're getting plenty of radiation now. Just a minute—Yeah, Dr. Hadamard, it's a bomb all right. But it hasn't got a fuse. Now how could they have made a fool mistake like that?"

"In other words, it's a dud," Joan said.

"That's right, a dud."

Now, at last, Braun wiped his face, which was quite gray. "I told you the truth," he said grimly. "My hunches don't work on stuff like this."

"But they do," I said. "I'm sorry we put you through the wringer—and you too, Colonel—but we couldn't let an opportunity like this slip. It was too good a chance for us to test how our facilities would stand up in a real bomb-drop."

"A real drop?" Anderton said. "Are you trying to say that CIG staged this? You ought to be shot, the whole pack of you!"

"No, not exactly," I said. "The enemy's responsible for the drop, all right. We got word last month from our man in Gdynia that they were going to do it, and that the bomb would be on board the *Ludmilla*. As I say, it was too good an opportunity to miss. We wanted to find out just how long it would take us to figure out the nature of the bomb— which we didn't know in detail—after it was dropped here. So we had our people in Gdynia defuse the thing after it was put on board the ship, but otherwise leave it entirely alone.

"Actually, you see, your hunch was right on the button as far as it went. We didn't ask you whether or not that object was a live bomb. We asked whether it was a bomb or not. You said it was, and you were right."

The expression on Braun's face was exactly like the one he had worn while he had been searching for his decision —except that, since his eyes were open, I could see that it was directed at me. "If this was the old days," he said in an ice-cold voice, "I might of made the Colonel's idea come true. I don't go for tricks like this, Pete."

"It was more than a trick," Clark put in. "You'll remember we had a deadline on the test, Mr. Braun. Obviously, in a real drop we wouldn't have all the time in the world to figure out what kind of a thing had been dropped. If we had still failed to establish that when the deadline ran out, we would have had to allow evacuation of the city, with all the attendant risk that that was exactly what the enemy wanted us to do."

"So?"

"So we failed the test," I said. "At one minute short of the deadline, Joan had the divers unscrew the cap. In a real drop that would have resulted in a detonation, if the bomb was real; we'd never risk it. That we did do it in the test was a concession of failure, an admission that our usual methods didn't come through for us in time.

"And that means that you were the only person who did come through, Mr. Braun. If a real bomb-drop ever comes, we're going to have to have you here, as an active part of our investigation. Your intuition for the one-shot gamble was the one thing that bailed us out this time. Next time it may save eight million lives."

There was quite a long silence. All of us, Anderton included, watched Braun intently, but his impassive face failed to show any trace of how his thoughts were running.

When he did speak at last, what he said must have seemed insanely irrelevant to Anderton, and maybe to Cheyney, too. And perhaps nothing more to Joan than the final clinical note in a case history.

"It's funny," he said, "I was thinking of running for Congress next year from my district. But maybe this is more important."

It was, I believe, the sigh of a man at peace with himself.

THE BOX

WHEN MEISTER got out of bed that Tuesday morning, he thought it was before dawn. He rarely needed an alarm clock these days—a little light in his eyes was enough to awaken him and sometimes his dreams brought him upright long before the sun came up.

It had seemed a reasonably dreamless night, but probably he had just forgotten the dreams. Anyhow, here he was, awake early. He padded over to the window, shut it, pulled up the blind and looked out.

The street lights were not off yet, but the sky was already a smooth, dark gray. Meister had never before seen such a sky. Even the dullest overcast before a snowfall shows some variation in brightness. The sky here—what he could see of it between the apartment houses—was like the inside of a lead helmet.

He shrugged and turned away, picking up the clock from the table to turn off the alarm. Some day, he promised himself, he would sleep long enough to hear it ring. That would be a good day; it would mean that the dreams were gone. In Concentration Camp Dora, one had awakened the moment the tunnel lights were put on; otherwise one might be beaten awake, or dead. Meister was deaf in the left ear on that account. For the first three days at Dora he had had to be awakened.

He became aware suddenly that he was staring fixedly at the face of the clock, his subconscious ringing alarm bells of its own. *Nine o'clock!* No, it was not possible. It was obviously close to sunrise. He shook the clock stupidly, although it was ticking and had been since he first noticed it. Tentatively he touched the keys at the back.

The alarm had run down.

This was obviously ridiculous. The clock was wrong. He put it back on the table and turned on the little radio. After a moment it responded with a terrific thrumming, as if a vacuum cleaner were imprisoned in its workings.

39

"B-flat," Meister thought automatically. He had only one good ear, but he still had perfect pitch—a necessity for a resonance engineer. He shifted the setting. The hum got louder. Hastily he reversed the dial. Around 830 kc, where WNYC came in, the hum was almost gone, but of course it was too early yet for the city station to be on the air—

". . . in your homes," a voice struck in clearly above the humming. "We are awaiting a report from Army headquarters. In the meantime, any crowding at the boundaries of of the barrier will interrupt the work of the Mayor's inquiry commission . . . Here's a word just in from the Port Authority: all ferry service has been suspended until further notice. Subways and tubes are running outbound trains only; however, local service remains normal so far."

Barrier? Meister went to the window again and looked out. The radio voice continued:

"NBC at Radio City disclaims all knowledge of the persistent signal which has blotted out radio programs from nine hundred kilocycles on up since midnight last night. This completes the roster of broadcasting stations in the city proper. It is believed that the tone is associated with the current wall around Manhattan and most of the other boroughs. Some outside stations are still getting through, but at less than a fiftieth of their normal input." The voice went on:

"At Columbia University, the dean of the Physics Department estimates that about the same proportion of sunlight is also getting through. We do not yet have any report about the passage of air through the barrier. The flow of water in the portions of the East and Hudson Rivers which lie under the screen is said to be normal, and no abnormalities are evident at the Whitehall Street tidal station."

There was a pause; the humming went on unabated. Then there was a sharp *beep!* and the voice said, "At the signal— 9 A.M., Eastern Daylight Savings Time."

Meister left the radio on while he dressed. The alarming pronouncements kept on, but he was not yet thoroughly disturbed, except for Ellen. She might be frightened; but probably nothing more serious would happen. Right now, he should be at the labs. If the Team had put this thing up overnight, they would tease him unmercifully for sleeping through the great event.

The radio continued to reel off special notices, warnings, new bulletins. The announcer sounded as if he were on the thin edge of hysteria; evidently he had not yet been told what it was all about. Meister was tying his left shoe when he realized that the reports were beginning to sound much worse.

"From LaGuardia Field we have just been notified that an experimental plane has been flown through the barrier at a point over the jammed Triboro Bridge. It has not appeared over the city and is presumed lost. On the *Miss New York* disaster early this morning we still have no complete report. Authorities on Staten Island say the ferry ordinarily carried less than two hundred passengers at that hour, but thus far only eleven have been picked up. One of these survivors was brought in to a Manhattan slip by the tub *Marjorie Q;* he is still in a state of extreme shock and Bellevue Hospital says no statement can be expected from him until tomorrow. It appears, however, that he swam *under* the barrier."

His voice carried the tension he evidently felt. "Outside the screen a heavy fog still prevails—the same fog which hid the barrier from the ferry captain until his ship was destroyed almost to the midpoint. The Police Department has again requested that all New Yorkers stay—"

Alarmed at last, Meister switched off the machine and left the apartment, locking it carefully. Unless those idiots turned off their screen, there would be panic and looting before the day was out.

Downstairs in the little grocery there was a mob arguing in low, terrified voices, their faces as gray as the ominous sky. He pushed through them to the phone.

The grocer was sitting behind it. "Phone service is tied up, Mr. Meister," he said hoarsely.

"I can get through, I think. What has happened?"

"Some foreign enemy, is *my* guess. There's a big dome of somethin' all around the city. Nobody can get in or out. You stick your hand in, you draw back a bloody stump. Stuff put through on the other side don't come through." He picked up the phone with a trembling hand and passed it over. "Good luck."

Meister dialed Ellen first. He needed to know if she were badly frightened, and to reassure her if she were. Nothing happened for a while; then an operator said, "I'm sorry, sir, but there will be no private calls for the duration of the emergency, unless you have a priority."

"Give me Emergency Code B-Nineteen, then," Meister said.

"Your group, sir?"

"Screen Team."

There was a faint sound at the outer end of the line, as if the girl had taken a quick breath. "Yes, sir," she said. "Right away." There was an angry crackle, and then the droning when the number was being rung.

"Screen Team," a voice said.

"Resonance section, please," Meister said, and when he was connected and had identified himself, a voice growled:

"Hello, Jake, this is Frank Schafer. Where the deuce are you? I sent you a telegram—but I suppose you didn't get it, the boards are jammed. Get on down here, quick!"

"No, I haven't any telegram," Meister said. "Whom do I congratulate?"

"Nobody, you fool! *We* didn't do this. We don't even know how it's been done!"

Meister felt the hairs on the back of his neck stirring. It was as if he were back in the tunnels of Concentration Camp Dora again. He swallowed and said, "But it is the antibomb screen?"

"The very thing." Schafer's tinny voice said bitterly. "Only somebody else has beat us to it—and we're trapped under it."

"It's really bombproof—you're sure of that?"

"It's anything-proof! Nothing can pass it! *And we can't get out of it, either!*"

It took quite a while to get the story straight. Project B-19, the meaningless label borne by the top-secret, billion-dollar Atomic Defense Project, was in turmoil. Much of its laboratory staff had been in the field or in Washington when the thing happened, and the jam in phone service had made it difficult to get the men who were still in the city back to the central offices.

"It's like this," Frank Schafer said, kneading a chunk of art gum rapidly. "This dome went up last night. It lets in a little light and a few of the strongest outside radio stations near by. But that's all—or anyhow, all that we've been able to establish so far. It's a perfect dome, over the whole island and parts of the other boroughs and New Jersey. It doesn't penetrate the ground or the water, but the only really big water frontage is way out in the harbor, so that lets out much chance of everybody swimming under it like that man from the *Miss New York*."

"The subways are running, I heard," Meister said.

"Sure; we can evacuate the city if we have to, but not fast enough." The mobile fingers crumbled bits off the sides of the art gum. "It won't take long to breathe up the air here, and if any fires start it'll be worse. Also there's a layer of ozone about twenty feet deep all along the inside of the barrier—but don't ask me why! Even if we don't have any big blazes, we're losing oxygen at a terrific rate by ozone-fixing and surface oxidization of the ionized area."

"Ionized?" Meister frowned. "Is there much?"

"Plenty!" Schafer said. "We haven't let it out, but in another twenty hours you won't be able to hear anything on the radio but a noise like a tractor climbing a pile of cornflakes. There's been an increase already. Whatever we're using for ether these days is building up tension fast."

A runner came in from the private wires and dropped a flimsy on Frank's desk. The physicist looked at it quickly, then passed it to Meister.

"That's what I figured. You can see the spot we're in."

The message reported that oxygen was diffusing inward through the barrier at about the same rate as might be accounted for by osmosis. The figures on loss of CO_2 were less easy to establish, but it appeared that the rate here was also of an osmotic order of magnitude. It was signed by a top-notch university chemist.

"Impossible!" Meister said.

"No, it's so. And New York is entirely too big a cell to live, Jake. If we're getting oxygen only osmotically, we'll be suffocated in a week. And did you ever hear of semipermeable membrane passing a lump of coal, or a tomato? Air, heat, food—all cut off."

"What does the Army say?"

"What they usually say: 'Do something, on the double!' We're lucky we're civilians, or we'd be court-martialed for dying!" Schafer laughed angrily and pitched the art gum away. "It's a very pretty problem, in a way," he said. "We have our antibomb screen. Now we have to find how to make ourselves *vulnerable* to the bomb—or cash in our chips. And in six days—"

The phone jangled and Schafer snatched at it. "Yeah, this is Dr. Schafer . . . I'm sorry, Colonel, but we have every available man called in now except those on the Mayor's commission . . . No, I don't know. Nobody knows, yet. We're tracing that radio signal now. If it has anything to do with the barrier, we'll be able to locate the generator and destroy it."

The physicist slammed the phone into its cradle and glared at Meister. "I've been taking this phone stuff all morning! I wish you'd showed up earlier. Here's the picture, briefly: The city is dying. Telephone and telegraph lines give us some communication with the outside, and we will be able to use radio inside the dome for a little while longer. There are teams outside trying to crack the barrier, but all the significant phenomena are taking place inside. Out there it just looks like a big black dome—no radiation effects, no ionization, no radio tone, no nothin'!

"We are evacuating now," he went on, "but if the dome stays up, over three quarters of the trapped people will die. If there's any fire or violence, almost all of us will die."

"You talk," Meister said, "as if you want me to kill the screen all by myself."

Schafer grinned nastily. "Sure, Jake! This barrier obviously doesn't act specifically on nuclear reactions; it stops almost everything. Almost everyone here is a nuclear man, as useless for this problem as a set of cooky-cutters. Every fact we've gotten so far shows this thing to be an immense and infinitely complicated form of cavity-resonance—and you're the only resonance engineer inside."

The grin disappeared. Schafer said, "We can give you all the electronics technicians you need, plenty of official backing, and general theoretical help. It's not much but it's all we've got. We estimate about eleven million people inside this box—eleven million corpses unless you can get the lid off it."

Meister nodded. Somehow, the problem did not weigh as heavily upon him as it might have. He was remembering Dora, the wasted bodies jammed under the stairs, in storerooms, fed into the bake-oven five at a time. One could survive almost anything if one had had practice in surviving. There was only Ellen—

Ellen was probably in The Box—the dome. That meant something, while eleven million was only a number.

"*Entdecken*," he murmured.

Schafer looked up at him, his blue eyes snapping sparks. Schafer certainly didn't look like one of the world's best nuclear physicists. Schafer was a sandy-haired runt—with the bomb hung over his head by a horsehair.

"What's that?" he said.

"A German word," Meister answered. "It means, to discover—literally, to take the roof off. That is the first step, it seems. To take the roof off, we must discover that transmitter."

"I've got men out with loop antennae. The geometrical center of the dome is right at the tip of the Empire State Building, but WNBT says there's nothing up there but their television transmitters."

"What they mean," Meister said, "is that there was nothing else up there two weeks ago. There *must* be a radiator at a radiant point no matter how well it is disguised."

"I'll send a team." Schafer got up, fumbling for the art gum he had thrown away. "I'll go myself, I guess. I'm jittery here."

"With your teeth? I would not advise it. You would die slain, as the Italians say!"

"Teeth?" Schafer said. He giggled nervously. "What's that got to—"

"You have metal in your mouth. If the mast is actually radiating this effect, your jawbones might be burnt out of your head. Get a group with perfect teeth, or porcelain fillings at best. And wear nothing with metal in it, not even shoes."

"Oh," Schafer said. "I knew we needed you, Jake." He rubbed the back of his hand over his forehead and reached into his shirt pocket for a cigarette.

Meister struck it out of his hand. "Six days' oxygen remaining," he said.

Schafer lunged up out of his chair, aimed a punch at Meister's head, and fainted across the desk.

The dim city stank of ozone. The street lights were still on. Despite radioed warnings to stay indoors surging mobs struggled senselessly toward the barrier. Counterwaves surged back, coughing, from the unbreathable stuff pouring out from it. More piled up in subway stations; people screamed and trampled one another. Curiously, the city's take that day was enormous. Not even disaster could break the deeply entrenched habit of putting a token in the turnstile.

The New York Central and Long Island Railroads, whose tracks were above ground where the screen cut across them, were shut down, as were the underground lines which came to the surface inside The Box. Special trains were running every three minutes from Pennsylvania Station, with passengers jamming the aisles and platforms.

In the Hudson Tubes the situation was worse. So great was the crush of fleeing humans there, they could hardly operate at all. The screen drew a lethal line between Hoboken and Newark, so that Tube trains had to make the longer of the two trips to get their passengers out of The Box. A brief power interruption stopped one train in complete darkness for ten minutes beneath the Hudson River, and terror and madness swept through it.

Queens and Brooklyn subways siphoned off a little pressure, but only a little. In a major disaster the normal human impulse is to go north, on the map-fostered myth that north is "up."

Navy launches were readied to ferry as many as cared to make the try out to where The Box lay over the harbor and the rivers, but thus far there were no such swimmers. Very few people can swim twenty feet under water, and to come up for air short of that twenty feet would be disastrous. That would be as fatal as coming up in the barrier itself; ozone is lung-rot in high concentrations. That alone kept most of the foolhardy from trying to run through the wall—that, and the gas-masked police cordon.

From Governor's Island, about half of which was in The Box, little Army ferries shipped over several cases of small arms which were distributed to subway and railroad guards. Two detachments of infantry also came along, relieving a little of the strain on the police.

Meister, hovering with two technicians and the helicopter pilot over a building on the edge of the screen, peered downward in puzzlement. It was hard to make any sense of the geometry of shadows below him.

"Give me the phone," he said.

The senior technician passed him the mike. A comparatively long-wave channel had been cleared by a major station for the use of emergency teams and prowl cars, since nothing could be heard on short-wave above that eternal humming.

"Frank, are you on?" Meister called. "Any word from Ellen yet?"

"No, but her landlady says she went to Jersey to visit yesterday," came over the air waves. There was an unspoken understanding between them that the hysterical attack of an hour ago would not be mentioned. "You'll have to crack

The Box to get more news, I guess, Jake. See anything yet?"

"Nothing but more trouble. Have you thought yet about heat conservation? I am reminded that it is summer; we will soon have an oven here."

"I thought of that, but it isn't so," Frank Schafer's voice said. "It seems hotter only because there's no wind. Actually, the Weather Bureau says we're *losing* heat pretty rapidly; they expect the drop to level at fifteen to twenty above."

Meister whistled. "So low! Yet there is a steady supply of calories in the water—"

"Water's a poor conductor. What worries me is this accursed ozone. It's diffusing through the city—already smells like the inside of a transformer around here!"

"What about the Empire State Building?"

"Not a thing. We ran soap bubbles along the power leads to see if something was tapping some of WNBT's power, but there isn't a break in them anywhere. Maybe you'd better go over there when you're through at the barrier. There are some things we can't make sense of."

"I shall," Meister said. "I will leave here as soon as I start a fire."

Schafer began to sputter. Meister smiled gently and handed the phone back to the technician.

"Break out the masks," he said. "We can go down now."

A rooftop beside the barrier was like some hell dreamed up in the violent ward of a hospital. Every movement accumulated a small static charge on the surface of the body, which discharged stingingly and repeatedly from the fingertips and even the tip of the nose if it approached a grounded object too closely.

Only a few yards away was the unguessable wall itself, smooth, deep gray, featureless, yet somehow quivering with a pseudo-life of its own—a shimmering haze just too dense to penetrate. It had no definite boundary. Instead, the tarpaper over which it lay here began to dim, and within a foot faded into the general mystery.

Meister looked at the barrier. The absence of anything upon which the eye could fasten was dizzying. The mind made up patterns and flashes of lurid color and projected them into the grayness. Sometimes it seemed that the fog extended for miles. A masked policeman stepped over from the inside parapet and touched him on the elbow.

"Wouldn't look at her too long, sir," he said. "We've

had ambulances below carting away sightseers who forgot to look away. Pretty soon your eyes sort of get fixed."

Meister nodded. The thing was hypnotic all right. And yet the eye was drawn to it because it was the only source of light here. The ionization was so intense that it bled off power from the lines, so that street lamps had gone off all around the edge. From the helicopter, the city had looked as if its rim was inked out in a vast ring. Meister could feel the individual hairs all over his body stirring; it made him feel infested. Well, there'd been no shortage of lice at Dora!

Behind him the technicians were unloading the apparatus from the 'copter. Meister beckoned. "Get a reading on field strength first of all," he said gloomily. "Whoever is doing this has plenty of power. Ionized gas, a difficult achievement—"

He stopped suddenly. Not so difficult. The city was enclosed; it was, in effect, a giant Geissler tube. Of course the concentration of rare gases was not high enough to produce a visible glow, but—

"Plenty high," the technician with the loop said, "Between forty-five and fifty thousand. Seems to be rising a little, too."

"Between—" Meister stepped quickly to the instrument. Sure enough, the black needle was wavering, so rapidly as to be only a fan-shaped blur between the two figures. "This is ridiculous! Is that instrument reliable?"

"I just took the underwriters' seal off it," the technician said. "Did you figure this much ozone could be fixed out without any alteration?"

"Yes, I had presupposed the equivalent of UV bombardment. This changes things. No wonder there is light leaking through that screen! Sergeant—"

"Yes sir?" the policeman mumbled through his mask.

"How much of the area below can you clear?"

"As much as you need."

"Good." Meister reached into his jacket pocket and produced the map of the city the pilot had given him. "We are here, yes? Make a cordon, then, from here to here." His soft pencil scrawled a black line around four buildings. "Then get as much fire-fighting equipment outside the line as you can muster."

"You're expecting a bad fire?"

"No, a *good* one. But hurry!"

The cop scratched his head in puzzlement, but he went

below. Meister smiled. Members of the Screen Team were the Mister Bigs in this city now. Twenty hours ago nobody'd ever heard of the Screen Team.

The technician, working with nervous quickness, was trying an oscilloscope into the loop circuit. Meister nodded approvingly. If there was a pulse to this phenomenon, it would be just as well to know its form. He snapped his fingers.

"What's wrong, doctor?"

"My memory. I have put my head on backwards when I got up this morning, I think. We will have to photograph the waveform; it will be too complex to analyze here."

"How do you know?" the technician asked.

"By that radio tone," Meister said. "You Americans work by sight. There are almost no resonance electronics men in this country. But in Germany we worked as much by ear as by eye. Where you convert a wave into a visible pattern, we turned it into an audible one. We had a saying that resonance engineers were disappointed musicians."

The face of the tube suddenly produced a green wiggle. It was the kind of wiggle a crazy man might make. The technician looked at it in dismay. "That," he said, "doesn't exist. I won't work in a science where it *could* exist!"

Meister grinned. "That is what I meant. The radio sound was a fundamental B-flat, but with hundreds of harmonics and overtones. You don't have it all in the field yet."

"I don't?" He looked. "So I don't! But when I reduce it that much, you can't see the shape of the modulations."

"We will have to photograph it by sections."

Bringing over the camera, the other man set it up. They worked rapidly, oppressed by the unnatural pearly glimmer, the masks, the stink of ozone which crept in at the sides of the treated cloth, the electrical prickling, above all by the silent terror of any trapped animal.

While they worked, the cop came back and stood by silently, watching. The gas mask gave no indication of his expression, but Meister could feel the pressure of faith radiating from the man. Doubtless these bits of equipment were meaningless to him—but bits of equipment like these had put up The Box, beyond the powers of policemen or presidents to take down again. Men who knew about such things were as good as gods now.

Unless they failed.

"That does it," the technician said.

The cop stepped forward. "I've got the area you marked roped off," he said diffidently. "We've searched the apartments and there's nobody in them. If there's any fire here, we'll be able to control it."

"Excellent!" Meister said. "Remember that this gas will feed the flames, however. You will need every possible man."

"Yes sir. Anything else?"

"Just get out of the district yourself."

Meister climbed into the plane and stood by the open hatch, looking at his wrist watch. He gave the cop ten minutes to leave the tenement and get out to the fire lines. Then he struck a match and pitched it out onto the roof.

"Up!" he shouted.

The rotors roared. The pitch on the roof began to smolder. A tongue of flame shot up. In three seconds the whole side of the roof nearest the gray screen was blazing.

The helicopter lurched and clawed for altitude.

Behind the plane arose a brilliant and terrifying yellow glare. Meister didn't bother to watch it. He squatted with his back to the fire and waved pieces of paper over the neck of a bottle.

The ammonia fumes were invisible and couldn't be smelled through the mask, but on the dry-plates wiggly lines were appearing. Meister studied them, nibbling gently at his lower lip. With luck, the lines would answer one question at least: they would tell what The Box was. With luck, they might even tell how it was produced.

They would *not* tell where it came from.

The motion of the 'copter changed suddenly, and Meister's stomach stirred uneasily under his belt. He stowed the plates and looked up. The foreshortened spire of the Empire State Building pointed up at him through the transparent deck; another 'copter hovered at its tip. The television antennae were hidden now in what seemed to be a globe of some dark substance.

Meister picked up the radio-phone. "Schafer?" he called—this to the Empire State Building.

"No, this is Talliafero," came back an answer. "Schafer's back at the labs. We're about ready to leave. Need any help?"

"I don't think so," Meister said. "Is that foil you have around the tower mast?"

"Yes, but it's only a precaution. The whole tower's radiating. The foil radiates, too, now that we've got it up. See you later."

The other 'copter stirred and swooped away.

Meister twisted the dial up into the short-wave region. The humming surged in; he valved down the volume and listened intently. The sound was different somehow. After a moment his mind placed it. The fundamental B-flat was still there, but some of the overtones were gone; that meant that hundreds of them, which the little amplifier could not reproduce, were also gone. He was listening on an FM set; his little table set at the apartment was AM. So the wave was modulated along both axes, and probably pulse-modulated as well. But why should it simplify as one approached its source?

Resonance, of course. The upper harmonics were echoes. Yet a simple primary tone in a well-known frequency range couldn't produce The Box by itself. It was the harmonics that made the difference, and the harmonics couldn't appear without the existence of some chamber like The Box. Along this line of reasoning, The Box was a precondition of its own existence. Meister felt his head swimming.

"Hey," the pilot said. "It's started to snow!"

Meister turned off the set and looked out. "All right, let's go home now."

Despite its depleted staff, the Screen Team was quiet with the intense hush of concentration that was its equivalent of roaring activity. Frank Schafer's door was closed, but Meister didn't bother to knock. He was on the edge of an idea and there was no time to be lost in formalities.

There were a number of uniformed men in the office with Frank. There was also a big man in expensive clothes, and a smaller man who looked as if he needed sleep. The smaller man had dark circles under his eyes, but despite his haggardness Meister knew him. The mayor. The big man did not look familiar—nor pleasant.

As for the high brass, nothing in a uniform looked pleasant to Meister. He pushed forward and put the dry-plates down on Schafer's desk. "The resonance products," he said. "If we can duplicate the fundamental in the lab——"

There came a roar from the big man. "Dr. Schafer, is this the man we've been waiting for?"

Schafer made a tired gesture. "Jake, this is Roland Dean," he said. "You know the mayor, I think. These others are security officers. They seem to think you made The Box."

Meister stiffened. "I? That's idiotic!"

"Any noncitizen is automatically under suspicion," one of the Army men said. "However, Dr. Schafer exaggerates. We just want to ask a few questions."

The mayor coughed. He was obviously tired, and the taint of ozone did not make breathing very comfortable.

"I'm afraid there's more to it than that, Dr. Meister," he added. "Mr. Dean here has insisted upon an arrest. I'd like to say for myself that I think it all quite stupid."

"Thank you," Meister said. "What is Mr. Dean's interest in this?"

"Mr. Dean," Schafer growled, "is the owner of that block of tenements you're burning out up north. The fire's spreading, by the way. When I told him I didn't know why you lit it, he blew his top."

"Why not?" Dean said, glaring at Meister. "I fail to see why this emergency should be made an excuse for irresponsible destruction of property. Have you any reason for burning my buildings, Meister?"

"Are you having any trouble with breathing, Mr. Dean?" Meister asked.

"Certainly! Who isn't? Do you think you can make it easier for us by filling The Box with smoke?"

Meister nodded. "I gather that you have no knowledge of elementary chemistry, Mr. Dean. The Box is rapidly converting our oxygen into an unbreathable form. A good hot fire will consume some of it, but it will also break up the ozone molecules. The ratio is about two atoms of oxygen consumed for every one set free—out of three which in the form of ozone could not have been breathed at all."

Schafer sighed gustily. "I should have guessed. A neat scheme, Jake. But what about the ratio between reduction of ozone and over-all oxygen consumption?"

"Large enough to maintain five of the six days' grace with which we started. Had we let the ozone-fixing process continue unabated, we should not have lasted forty hours longer."

"Mumbo jumbo!" Dean said stonily, turning to Schafer. "A halfway measure. The problem is to get us out of this mess, not to stretch our sufferings out by three days by invading property rights. This man is a German, probably a Nazi! By your own admission, he's the only man in your whole section who's seemed to know what to do. And nothing he's done so far has shown any result, except to destroy some of my buildings!"

"Dr. Meister, just what *has* been accomplished thus far?" a colonel of Intelligence said.

"Only a few tentative observations," Meister said. "We have most of the secondary phenomena charted."

"Charts!" Dean snorted.

"Can you offer any assurance that The Box will be down in time?" the colonel asked.

"That," Meister said, "would be very foolish of me. The possibility exists, that is all. Certainly it will take time—we have barely scratched the surface."

"In that case, I'm afraid you'll have to consider yourself under arrest—"

"See here, Colonel!" Schafer surged to his feet, his face flushed. "Don't you know that he's the only man in The Box who can crack it? That fire was good common sense. If you arrest my men for *not* doing anything, we'll never get anything done!"

"I am not exactly stupid, Dr. Shafer," the colonel said harshly. "I have no interest in Mr. Dean's tenements, and if the mayor is forced to jail Dr. Meister we will spring him at once. All I'm interested in is the chance that Dr. Meister may be *maintaining* The Box instead of trying to *crack it*."

"Explain, please," Meister said mildly.

Pulling himself up to military straightness, the colonel cleared his throat and said:

"You're inside The Box. If you put it up, you have a way out of it, and know where the generator is. You may go where you please, but from now on we'll have a guard with you. . . . Satisfied, Dr. Schafer?"

"It doesn't satisfy me!" Dean rumbled. "What about my property? Are you going to let this madman burn buildings with a guard to help?"

The colonel looked at the landlord. "Mr. Dean," he said quietly, "you seem to think The Box was created to annoy you personally. The Army hasn't the technical knowledge to destroy it, but it has sense enough to realize that more than just New York is under attack here. The enemy, whoever he may be, thinks his screen uncrackable, otherwise he wouldn't have given us this chance to work on it by boxing in one city alone. If The Box is not down in, say, eight days, he'll know that New York failed and died—and every city in the country will be bombed to slag the next morning."

Schafer sat down again, looking surly. "Why?" he asked the army man. "Why would they waste the bombs when they could just box in the cities?"

"Inefficient. America's too big to occupy except slowly, piecemeal. They'd have no reason to care if large parts of it were uninhabitable for a while. The important thing is to knock us out as a military force, as a power in world affairs."

"If they boxed in all the cities at once—"

The colonel shook his head. "We have rocket emplacements of our own, and they *aren't* in large cities. Neither Box nor bomb would catch more than a few of them. No. They have to know that The Box is uncrackable, so they can screen their own cities against our bombs until our whole country is knocked out. With The Box, that would take more than a week, and their cities would suffer along with ours. With bombs, a day would be enough. So they've allowed us this test. If New York comes out of this, there'll be no attack, at least until they've gotten a better screen. The Box seems good enough so far!"

"Politics," Schafer said, shaking his head disgustedly. "It's much too devious for me! Doesn't The Box constitute an attack?"

"Certainly—but who's doing the attacking?" the colonel demanded. "We can guess, but we don't know. And I doubt very much that the enemy has left any traces."

Meister stiffened suddenly, a thrill of astonishment shooting up his backbone. Schafer stared at him.

"Traces!" Meister said. "Of course! That is what has been stopping us all along. Naturally there would be no traces. We have been wasting time looking for them. Frank, the generator is not in the Empire State Building. *It is not even in The Box!*"

"But, Jake, it's got to be," Schafer said. "It's physically impossible for it to be outside!"

"A trick," Dean rumbled.

Meister waved his hands excitedly. "No, no! This is the reasoning which has made our work so fruitless. Observe. As the colonel says, the enemy would not dare leave traces. Now, workmanship is traceable, particularly if the device is revolutionary, as this one is. Find that generator and you know at once which country has made it. You observe the principle, and you say to yourself, 'Ah, yes, there were reports, rumors, whispers of shadows of rumors of such a principle, but I discounted them as fantasy; they came out of Country X.' Do you follow?"

"Yes, but—"

"But no country would leave such a fingerprint where it could be found. This we can count upon. Whereas we know as yet next to nothing about the physics of The Box. Therefore, if it is physically impossible for the generator to be outside The Box, this does not mean that we must continue to search for it inside. It means that we must find a physical principle which makes it possible to be outside!"

Frank Schafer threw up his hands. "Revise basic physics in a week! Well, let's try. I suppose Meister's allowed lab work, Colonel?"

"Certainly, as long as my guards aren't barred from the laboratory."

Thirty hours later the snow stopped falling, leaving a layer a little over three inches deep. The battling mobs were no longer on the streets. Hopeless masses were jammed body to body in railroad stations and subways. The advancing ozone had driven the people in upon themselves, and into the houses and basements where rooms could be sealed against the searing stench.

Thousands had already died along the periphery. The New Jersey and Brooklyn shores were charnel heaps of those who had fought to get back across the river to Manhattan and cleaner air. The tenements along the West Side of the island still blazed,—twenty linear blocks of them,—but the fire had failed to jump Ninth Avenue and was dying for want of fuel. Elsewhere it was very cold. The city was dying.

Over it, The Box was invisible. It was the third night.

In the big lab at the Team Office, Meister, Schafer, and the two technicians suddenly disappeared under a little Box of their own, leaving behind four frantic soldiers. Meister sighed gustily and looked at the black screen a few feet from his head.

"Now we know," he said. "Frank, you can turn on the light now."

The desk lamp clicked on. In the shaded glow Meister saw that tears were trickling down Schafer's cheeks.

"No, no, don't weep yet, the job is not quite done!" Meister cried. "But see—so simple, so beautiful!" He gestured at the lump of metal in the exact center of the Boxed area. "Here we are—four men, a bit of metallic trash, an empty desk, a lamp, a cup of foil. Where is the screen generator? Outside!"

Schafer swallowed. "But it isn't," he said hoarsely. "Oh, you were right, Jake—the key projector *is* outside. But it doesn't generate the screen; it just excites the iron there, and that does the job." He looked at the scattered graphs on the desk top. "I'd never have dreamed such a jam of fields was possible! Look at those waves—catching each other, heterodyning, slowing each other up as the tension increases. No wonder the whole structure of space gives way when they finally get in phase!"

One of the technicians looked nervously at the little Box and cleared his throat. "I still don't see why it should leak light, oxygen, and so forth, even the little that it does. The jam has to be radiated away, and the screen should be the subspatial equivalent of a perfect radiator, a black body. But it's gray."

"No, it's black," Schafer said. "But it isn't turned on all the time. If it were, the catalyst radiation couldn't get through. It's a perfect electromagnetic push-me-pull-you. The apparatus outside projects the catalyst fields in. The lump of iron— in this case the Empire State Building—is excited and throws off the screen fields. The screen goes up. The screen cuts off the catalyst radiation. The screen goes down. In comes the primary beam again. And so on. The kicker is that without the off-again-on-again, you wouldn't get anything—the screen couldn't exist because the intermittence supplies some· of the necessary harmonics."

He grinned ruefully. "Here I am explaining it as if I understood it. You're a good teacher, Jake!"

"Once one realizes that the screen has to *be* up before it can *go* up," Meister said, grinning back, "one has the rest— or most of it. Introducing a rhythmic interruption of the very first pulses is a simple trick. The hardest thing about it is timing—to know just when the screen goes up for the first time, so that the blinker can be cut out at precisely that moment."

"So how do we get out?"

"Feedback," Meister said. "There must be an enormous back EMF in the incoming beam. And whether it is converted and put back into the system again at the source, or just efficiently wasted, we can burn it out." He consulted a chalk line which ran along the floor from the edge of the little

Box to the lump of iron, then picked up the cup of foil and pointed it along the mark away from the lump. "The trick," he said soberly, "is not to nullify, but to amplify—"

The glare of the overheads burst in upon them. The lab was jammed with soldiers, all with rifles at the ready and all the rifles pointing in at them. The smell of burned insulation curled from an apparatus at the other end of the chalk line.

"Oh," said Schafer. "We forgot the most important thing! Which way does our chalk line run from the Empire State Building, I wonder?"

"It could be anywhere above the horizon," Meister said. "Try pointing your reflector straight up, first."

Schafer swore. "Any time you want a diploma for unscrewing the inscrutable, Jake," he said, "I'll write you one with my nose!"

It was cold and quiet now in the city. The fires on the West Side, where one of the country's worst slums had been burned out, smoldered and flickered.

The air was a slow, cumulative poison. It was very dark.

On top of the Empire State Building a great, shining bowl swung in a certain direction, stopped, waited. Fifty miles above it, in a region where neither *cold* nor *air* have any human meaning, a clumsy torpedo began to warm slightly. Inside it, delicate things glowed, fused—melted. There was no other difference; the torpedo kept on, traveled at its assigned twenty-one and eight-tenths miles per minute. It would always do so.

The Box vanished. The morning sunlight glared in. There was a torrent of rain as cold air hit hot July. Within minutes the city was as gray as before, but with roiling thunderheads. People poured out of the buildings into the downpour, hysterical faces turned to the free air, shouting amid the thunder, embracing each other, dancing in the lightning flares.

The storm passed almost at once, but the dancing went on quite a while.

"Traces!" Meister said to Frank Schafer. "Where else could you hide them? An orbital missile was the only answer."

"That sunlight," Schafer said, "sure looks good! You'd better go home to bed, Jake, before the official hero-worshipers catch up with you."

But Meister was already dreamlessly asleep.

FIRST STRIKE

I DON'T THINK I'm going to like logging as a trade, but on the other hand I don't have much of a choice. The one profession I really know can't be practiced these days in the United States, and I don't care to practice it for the benefit of any other country, not even Canada. Besides, I'm supposed to be dead—and I'm going to stay dead until Carol gets up here.

Not that she's going to like my being a logger, any better than she liked my being a rocket pilot. The joke was on her, for there was supposed to be nothing she liked better than "roughing it." I should know; I roughed it with her all the way up to the day before spaceflight.

Not that there was any chance of her understanding either spaceflight or rocketry, as she had been at pains to make clear to me at once when I'd been assigned to the High Altitude Project. It was just that the job gave her a difficult row to hoe socially. Rocketry and spaceflight were both high on the social leprosy list, even in those days. All during the course of the Project we'd had to endure watching our erstwhile friends fall away from us; first the embarrassed, determinedly general conversation, then the forgoten date and the silent telephone, and at last, the cut direct.

By the time the evening for the farewell party came around, there was no one left but Jim and Dorothy McLaughlin—whom, of course, we could have counted on. Jim and Dot are salt and soil; the essential kind of people, the kind that keeps humanity going through its periodic idiocies.

All the same, it was a gloomy sort of party. After dinner we sat around for what seemed like hours, until it became obvious that nobody else was coming. You know the old saw —when everybody in a party falls silent at once, an angel is passing over the house. The traffic was heavy over our summer shelter that night.

"What's the schedule for tomorrow?" Jim said at last. "I

suppose you're all tooled up by now, since the flight's scheduled for the day after."

"More or less," I said. "All the essential details of the firing were set up months ago, of course. And as far as the mechanisms of the missile are concerned—well, they'll either work or they won't. They've been checked under resistance loads and so on a thousand times, and we'll be constantly rechecking until the last minute, but we don't expect to find anything wrong. How they'll behave against actual flightloads, instead of just resistances, is up for betting."

"Doesn't that leave you a day free, then, Wally?" Dot said. I could see that she was uneasy, despite her loyalty. As with Carol, the whole subject, like any subject connected with science, was frightening to her.

"No, Dot, it doesn't. You see, we still have to go through about 38 meaningless motions for the benefit of the public."

"But why?"

"Because they're scared. Hell, Dot, *you're* scared. You and they want to be told we aren't tampering with something that's going to hurt them. It's silly, but it's the way people feel."

"I don't know that it's so silly," Jim said slowly. "We've gotten to a point now where science seems to be paying us off in tragedy rather than in real profits. It began back at Hiroshima and it's been getting worse since."

"That's not true, but I know why you think it is. The Old Master and his ilk have done a pretty thorough job." The Old Master, of course, was the writer who had died that year; the man who had regaled the public with hundreds of stories about Mars, out of an abysmal ignorance of the probable actualities of that planet, but with a personal style which seemed to find no saturation point in most people. "For the past five years, all the most popular science fiction writers have been teaching their readers that the results of any scientific advance are automatically and entirely horrible. Now those readers believe it. Why shouldn't they? They take the science fiction writers to be the only interpreters of science they have, which may even be so. These days we're getting the same thesis from the pulpit and even from Congress."

"I think they're right," Dot said. "What good does it do us to know about the atom if it just blows us up in the long run? And why are we trying to get into space anyhow? There's nothing out there but a lot of nothing, and some balls of rock nobody wants. I think science at least ought to call a holiday and let us catch up with it a bit."

"Now where have I heard that before?"

"So it's old," Jim said defensively. "But maybe it's no worse than a lot of old ideas. Maybe there *is* a point of diminishing returns for science. Or maybe we've just emphasized science too heavily. For instance, Wally, I think you're unfair to the Old Master. All he meant to do was to show the dangers of *over*emphasis on technology. He didn't attack all science—his imitators and his fans misinterpreted him."

"Maybe," I said. "I've seen a couple of quotations from his own lips that make me think his imitators and his fans had his intentions dead to rights. If they're to be censured, it's for letting him do their thinking for them, not for misinterpreting him."

"What does it matter?" Carol said. "I'm tired of science, myself. I think it's going to lose me a husband day after tomorrow, unless I'm lucky. That's enough to make *me* dislike it."

"Exactly so," Jim said, with great seriousness. "Wally, let me ask you this, why are you going?"

"Somebody has to go," I said. "I happen to have the training."

"*Why* does somebody have to go?"

I throttled down my temper. "Because there's a place to go to. Because the whole process of increasing knowledge is irreversible. Because I personally want to know what it's like out in space, and on the planets."

"In short, irresponsible curiosity—the same irresponsible curiosity that gave us the atom bomb."

"You obviously know damned little about the atom bomb," I said. "If the Manhattan Project was 'irresponsible curiosity' then so was Pasteur's study of wine fermentation."

"Now wait a minute," Jim said stiffly. "There was a practical end in view there. He was hired by the wine people to save their product."

"All right, go back to Spallanzani. He had no practical end in view. All he wanted to find was whether or not bacteria arose by spontaneous generation, or had parents like the rest of us. Pure research—'irresponsible curiosity.' Have you ever been sick, Jim?"

"Sure. I had typhus while I was in the Middle East with the Navy. I was sick, plus."

"Why didn't you die?"

"They gave me some antibiotic or other," Jim said slowly. "There are so many, it's hard to keep track of them. All right, I see your point. Now you see mine. Spallanzini's discovery was biological. It led by a long road to the antibiotics. It dealt with life, and it saved lives. But how do physics or astronomy expect to save lives and lives and make things better for poor damn fools like me? Am I happier because the physicists discovered the atom bomb? The hell I am. Am I going to be happier after you characters get your rocket into space? No, sir. I'm just going to have still another menace hanging over my head."

"Oh, for God's sake," I said. "Look, Jim, an orbital rocket is no menace, to you or anybody else, not now, not with the political setup the way it is. Years ago it would have been used as a bomb-launching platform, that I'll grant you. But I don't see any chance that it'll be needed for that now. Where's the danger?"

"What goes up must come down," Carol said complacently, working her knitting needles and squinting in the candlelight.

"That's not true!"

"Don't you shout at me, Wally Swain."

"Carol's right," Dot said. "Who wants to have a couple of tons of electronic junk hanging miles above their heads for the rest of their lives? Talk about the Sword of Damocles!"

I stood up. "I don't think this is getting us any place," I said. "I'm going. I'm under orders to go, for one thing. For another, I want to go. In the long run nothing else can happen. Why not grow up and face it?"

Jim rose after me, his face flinty in the dim, uneasy light.

"It may be inevitable, Wally," he said. "But I don't have to like it. I think it ought to be stopped. You engineering boys have been hot-rodding it back and forth over us ordinary people for a long time. If we're not sick of it by now, we deserve anything we get."

We looked at each other. Somehow what I saw didn't look much like Jim McLaughlin any more. The face was Jim McLaughlin, but the eyes were Peking Man. I felt Carol's hand on my arm, but it didn't help much.

Jim and Dot were salt and soil—basically decent, the best in the long run that Earth had to offer. I loved them both. But I was more than ready to take the first step toward another planet. . . .

The next morning I got out of bed feeling as if my sinuses had been packed with rockwool. It was pitch black. I groped for the candlestick and struck a match. Nothing happened. I swore and struck it again. This time it lit, with a terrific sputtering, a cloud of white smoke, and a vile smell.

Carol stirred protestingly. "Wally," she said. "Can't you finish a sentence without swearing?"

"All right. All the same this is the last goddamned morning I cope with these candles. Every last one of them goes out of the house today and tomorrow I'm having electricity run in here."

"You say that every day," Carol said lazily. "Besides, tomorrow you'll be shooting all over the sky in your toy. Hurry up and light the candle, dear, before you burn your fingers."

She was a little late. In grim silence I struck another match twice and lit the candle. Last night, after the party, I had carefully placed a half dozen packs of her matches on the bedside table, but somehow I had scooped up a pack of my own along with them, and that had to be the pack I'd hit that morning. Damn roughing it, anyhow.

I put on the bright plaid woolose shirt with the lieutenant's bars, and struggled into my plastidenim dungarees. They were not new, but they remained an offensive, faded-type blue. No amount of mistreatment had changed their color or worked the creases out of them.

Having converted myself into a reasonable, hand-drawn caricature of an officer and a gentleman by act of Congress, I felt my way across the bedroom and unpolarized the windows. Carol covered her eyes pointedly as the bright sunlight came in.

"I'm sorry," I said. "If I could move the dial over beside the bed, I could let the sun in before you woke up—and I wouldn't have to fuss with that goddamn candle."

"Anything to do things differently from the way normal people do them," she said. "You're the man who used to complain that people wouldn't let themselves become aware of what kind of a world they'd have to live in after the atomic war. Now that they're actually trying to train themselves to live under those conditions, you only grouse louder."

"But there's no longer any need—" I began. Then, "Oh, the hell with it! I've got to go. Are you coming out to the base today?"

"No, I'm going to archery practice with the wives."

"Okay. Don't wing any more Dobermans. The government doesn't pay me enough to survive two lawsuits in one year."

The knotted door squealed as I opened it. There was nothing wrong with the door; the squeal was attached to it in a little box, and the knots were paint.

I climbed on my motorbike and jolted toward the base over the rundown road. Our summer shelter was located in a discouraged forest of scrub and regrowth, about halfway between the base and the suburbs of the nearest large town. This was the best compromise we had been able to make. Being closer to the town would have meant less roughing it than Carol wanted, and being closer to the base would have meant more than she wanted. That kind of compromise.

Just how much "shelter" our so-called shelter would have provided in the event of an actual atomic raid was not even an open question. Like all summer shelters, it was really a flimsy affair. But that didn't matter.

During the Cold War of 1950–62, as Carol had reminded me, most Americans allowed themselves to be pushed about by the civil defense authorities without the slightest emotional conviction that any thing might happen to *them*. A few businessmen moved their bonds and records out of large cities, and some even bought concrete retreats in remote sections of Maine, but there had been nothing like any general preparation for survival at the level of the individual—nor any industrial decentralization, either. I do remember one exception—a New York showgirl who left the city to escape the Bomb and built herself a cozy retreat in militarily uninteresting country near White Sands, New Mexico . . .

When the Cold War was abruptly called off, with the Partition of Europe in May 1961, the Soviet Union underwent a rather noisy change of government. After that, the threat of serious hostilities evaporated. Then, suddenly my fellow citizens went into spasms of what was supposed to be preparedness. Something about the barbaric post-Bomb world, of which they had so often been warned without result, belatedly caught at their imaginations and thinking in terms of it became a parlor game. Worse, it became a fashion in living. Commuters vied with each other in being earthy and red-blooded. The newspapers ran long, unlikely articles on how to survive in a collapsed civilization. "Going back to the soil" was talked about and back-lot vegetable gardens overflowed onto front lawns in all the best suburbs.

The waterproof matches were a typical sample. Presumably the post-Bomb world for which we pretended to be preparing was to be one in which we were going to be sopping wet most of the time. The matches were made by being dipped in water-glass or some similar substance. It took two scratches to light one. The first scratch got the sodium silicate off the tip, the second lit the match itself.

In the new barbarism, it was tacitly assumed, women would be largely helpless and would exist to be dragged prettily about by the hair, by the men. Consequently women didn't have to carry the stinking waterproof matches; all match folders were plainly marked "Hisn" or "Hern," depending on what kind they were. (Mangled English also was widely affected, as a sign its user was rough-and-ready.)

I was ready to admit that this invention had brought about at least one social gain. For years I had been accusing Carol of never having matches of her own. The division of match folders into genders proved it to her, and even had produced some small improvement. She hated that stench of the waterproof tabs as much as I did, could never get them to light, and, since there was no pressure of custom on her to carry them, she remembered to bring her own about 32 per cent of the time.

The rocket—the orbital missile, to be precise—came into sight as I left the scrub oaks behind. It was beautiful: pure, unencumbered, sexless, and implicit with the ultimate freedom. It was like Brancusi's *Bird in Space* given function. I loved it.

I went to the barracks rather than to the launching dugout, in order to stay out of sight of Brigadier General Wallingford-Kentworth, ostensible director of the project. Actually the missile was the joint baby of the Navy, the Weather Bureau, the Bureau of Standards, and the FSA Satellite Vehicle Program, none of them having much love for the Army. The general was a political appointee. The real head of the project was *the* Dr. Helmuth Eisenwald, a civilian garnered many years before from Aberdeen, and before that from Peenemünde. I knew he would be in the barracks, for the same reason that I was going there.

"Hi, Doc."

"Good morning, Wally. Are you all tuned up for tomorrow?"

"Tuned up? My God, Doc, I can't wait for it. I only wish we were really going to the Moon. The newspapers have us practically there already."

"The newspapers," Eisenwald said, his mouth taking on a German shape. "If it were not for them, we would all be home in bed getting a little of necessary rest. All this fakery makes me want to vomit."

"You haven't lived here long enough. The fakery's essential. Have you heard about the Church of Gifts Held Back?"

Eisenwald shrugged, a gesture through which he was able to convey several hundred different meanings at will. "We have been through this religious business before. The Inquisition made Galilei recant, but Jupiter continues to have satellites. In this country evolution is even taught in Tennessee, in spite of a state law repealing Darwin's observations. Besides, Wally, the brigadier general has surrounded the base with marines; how many divisions can the Fundamentalists muster?"

"That isn't the point, Doc. I'm as sure as you are that superstition can't stop our ship. But what about the ship after that—the one that's supposed to bring me supplies, and start the construction of the station? Wouldn't I look silly hanging in an orbit 1,075 miles straight up from here, waiting for another ship that never arrived?"

"That could not happen," Eisenwald said, alarmed. "The second missile is already half built."

"Half. You have no conception of the speed and the accuracy with which our Congress can reflect current idiocy. Way down at the bottom of the public mind there's always a strong current of common sense, but somehow it never finds its way to Washington. Oh, well, the hell with it. I'll let physics get me up there, and if the senators won't legislate me down again, I'll spit on their bald spots every time I pass over Washington. Now then, what are the actual launching arrangements?"

I could tell by Eisenwald's expression that I had been talking too fast for him; he blinked twice before his mind seized gratefully upon the concrete query. "Let's go out to the ship," he said. "This barracks is too crowded."

An empty gallium tanker was being towed away from the ship as we crossed the field. There was otherwise not a great deal of activity.

"The actual firing you will do, of course," Eisenwald said, "But you will do it at a signal from outside. That is why we installed ship-to-ground television."

I paused on the ladder and looked down at him. "Wouldn't a simple light or sound signal, or even the ship's clock, have been enough?"

"No, because clock firing time is slightly flexible, and because you must be able to see the launching ceremony and judge for yourself what is the most convincing moment to push the key. That's why we gave you test for deception—had you not wondered?"

"Yes," I said, ducking through the airlock and reaching down a hand to him. "I couldn't see that there'd be anybody for me to deceive, all by myself out in orbit. I was about convinced that the Army wanted me to broadcast phony reports back to Earth while in flight."

"They may yet decide just that," Eisenwald said soberly. He sat down on a stanchion; I sprawled in the acceleration hammock. "I've heard rumors to that effect, at least. But there is a more important reason. We are trying to make this orbital rocket seem simple and understandable and peaceable to your laymen, to channel off as much of this antiscientific hysteria as possible. One of the arrangements which we have made is to make it seem that the rocket is started from outside. Your psychologists tell me that of all our deceptions, that one is the most important. In an hysterical matriarchy, the rocket is a symbol with sexual overtones and therefore must not seem self-starting. If that deception fails, the others will. It will act as a trigger. So it must go as planned—or, as you say, there may well be no second missile for many years."

"There's got to be," I said. "Other people are working on space travel. We're up to it technologically now, and we've got to strike for it now. If we're prevented by our own cumulative ignorance, somebody else will get in the first strike. . . . Well, what is the exact arrangement, Doc?"

Eisenwald smiled paternally. "That I choose not to tell you," he said. "As long as we had to install this video set, I have decided to put it to use in a small pleasantry for your benefit. A little, harmless ceremony, a fitting one, to send you off. I have told you all you really need to know; let the rest be my surprise."

"Of course, Doc. You're a sentimentalist, aren't you? I am, too, about the ship anyhow."

He smiled again. "I think you are needed no more today, Wally. I see no point in your drifting around the base just in the hope of being helpful. Some corporal might set you to policing the area. Since you need rest, I dismiss you."

"Thanks, Doc." I thought about it. The acceleration hammock was comfortable, and the instrument-jeweled walls around me were beautiful. I thought about Carol, and the door with the built-in squeak, and the candlestick, and the summer shelter. Tomorrow I'd be gone—gone out, really out of a world which made no sense. I'd be back, of course—but if my luck held, only to go out again, farther, and more finally.

"I'll stick around here," I said. "I'll use the time to make myself at home in the cabin. There couldn't be such a thing as being too familiar with it. You could send me in a farewell dinner, and I'll give the disposal converter a try with the ship sealed. And I'll sleep in the hammock, too. At that I'll need practice."

"But Wally—your wife?"

I thought about salt and soil, and then about Peking Man —and Woman. I loved them, but all of a sudden I'd grown up.

"I'd about decided to do this, last night," I said, and I think it was true. "We made our real farewells this morning. If you'd phone her for me and tell her that I'm staying here as planned, I'd appreciate it. Frankly, I'm feeling a bit washed out. I'd just as soon not go through a second farewell scene. Bad for her, as well as for me."

He showed complete and most satisfying misunderstanding. Doc was the one man in the world I hated to lie to, but some things are and must remain personal.

"That's most wise," he said. He seemed pleased. "All right, my friend. I will make my farewells here, also. Good luck."

We shook hands. His eyes were moist. Mine may have been, too.

I slept very comfortably in the hammock, and it was luxurious to be able to get light in the morning just by pushing a button right above the end of my nose. Nothing had changed; the walls glittered all around me. But why should anything have changed? Here was where I belonged, in a chamber I would never leave if I had my druthers. I was a born rocketeer. The tests had shown it, and I could feel it in every cell of my body.

I ate and generally made myself ready, then looked at the clock. It wouldn't be long now. Down below I could hear the humming of the secondary generator, which provided the power to pull the damping rods out of the pile so that the pile itself could take over. While I listened it died, and the sound of the pile-driven primary began to whine up and up. Somebody was readying the ship from the small emergency board on the outside of the hull. That was considerate of somebody—Doc Eisenwald, no doubt.

The speaker said, "Wally, are you there?"

"I'm here, Doc. I'll take over now. Thanks for letting me snooze this long."

"You needed it. But now I have a newspaperman who wants to speak to you."

"I've already been interviewed 4,000—oh, well, put him on."

The television screen lit up and a long, shrewd face stared at me. I stared back.

"Lieutenant Swain, I'm Bill Forehan, representing the wire service pool. We understand that you spent the night in the rocket, to get used to living in it. Is that right?"

"That's right."

"Would you tell us how it felt?"

"Cozy," I said.

"You had no trouble getting to sleep?"

"No, not a bit. The hammock is pretty thick and soft."

The newsman nodded. "Has to be, of course. No other sensations? Any feeling of being in space already?"

"No, not really. The gravity is too real to ignore. Of course I had a daydream or two, I'll admit."

That was the right note. The reporter could take it from there to the colleagues he represented and they all could evolve romantic, self-contradictory speeches for me to have made, to their hearts' content. He nodded again and went away.

As he left the screen I could see, for the first time, the crowd beyond. It was hostile and frightened. I had had no idea how scared it would be.

Two grease monkeys were walking along the concrete trough that led from the base of the rocket to the launching dugout, several hundred feet away. They were pouring something into the trough, something that dusted gently in the early morning wind. Beyond the dugout, a long way beyond, was a high wire fence, heavily patrolled by marines. Behind the fence was a deep trench filled with coils of barbed wire, and behind that was another fence.

Behind that fence was the crowd.

It muttered constantly, and there was a lot of catcalling. Farther back still, there was a sort of nucleus of disquiet, in the middle of which a tall figure stood out above the other heads, waving its arms wildly and shouting in apocalyptic tones. Now and then the crowd around it would shout back. I could see several men with medical department brassards pushing toward the preacher, one of them carrying a rolled-up stretcher like a spear. Evidently the fanatic already had succeeded in scaring somebody into convulsions.

I switched the scene out to take a look at the inside of the launching dugout. Speeches were already in progress and had been for some time. Eisenwald had spared me most of them. The big P.A. speakers atop the second fence had given the crowd the whole stifling dose, however. As for the talk still remaining, I had the comfort of knowing that all speeches *had* to end by a given moment on the clock, and that that moment was not far off.

Among the group in the dugout I could pick out Carol. I hadn't expected her to be among the elect group, but I wasn't too surprised; Doc was a sentimentalist. Her face was extremely white and drawn. She'd taken my night in the cabin hard, of course; and besides, being terrified of rockets was integral to roughing it. Her expression made me feel a little funny.

Well, good-bye to all that. Up, up, and away, as the character in the cape used to say.

After Wallingford-Kentworth had run down, the announcer came on again and introduced Eisenwald as a man who needed no introduction, which was true. Doc's voice was heavy, and trembling a little. Partly he was playing the role required of him, telling the lies that needed to be told, but much of the emotion was real.

"Ladies and gentlemen," he said. "As you probably all know, the rocket will be fired from here. The method is very simple. Lieutenant Swain, inside the rocket—are you there, Wally?"

"Sure am, Doc," I said. Behind the dugout, facing the crowd, a big projection screen was showing a brief flash of me at the controls, grinning a confident, all-American grin. It had been taken on film weeks ago; without it, the crowd wouldn't have believed I was really in the rocket.

"Good for you. Lieutenant Swain, ladies and gentlemen, will release a small quantity of his fuel into the concrete pit you see right under the rocket, at the other end of this concrete trench, and will prime his engines. In the trench is a train of powder, which will be lighted right here, in the launching dugout. The light will travel down the trench to the pit, where it will fire the excess fuel and start Lieutenant

Swain's engines. In short, what we have here is essentially a Fourth of July skyrocket with a long fuse, differing only in size from those with which you are all familiar—"

So that was it. Since my "fuel"—that is, the reaction-mass the heat of the pile would shove out the jets—was gallium vapor, no possible powder flame could ever set it on fire; it ran at a flat 2000° C. And the "concrete pit" Doc was talking about was actually the mouth of a long tunnel, leading to a 200-foot stack a mile away. Only after they had traveled that distance would the hot isotopes of the blast have cooled down enough to make it safe to release them on the air.

But I had to admit that it was a convincing dodge for the public, which had been kept carefully ignorant of science for so many years by the antiscience fiction purveyors.

I could also see the reason for the ship-to-ground telescreen. I had to be able to see just when the powder train was touched off and to judge its rate of progress. On the clock were two red marks, one on either side of the zero point, a total of fifteen seconds apart. Any take-off made within that fifteen-second period would be good; the ship's computer would trim the flight to the split second.

"Now, ladies and gentlemen, we would like to introduce to you the most heroic woman of our time—a woman whose heroism is matched only by that of her husband. Mrs. Swain, would you come forward, please?"

She came forward. Something began to disturb me. I didn't then quite know what it was.

"Mrs. Swain, you are making an immense sacrifice for the sake of the whole human race. We want you to know that the world honors you today in equal measure with your husband. No human being, no government, has the right to compel such a sacrifice; no nation has the right to impose upon a citizen a parting with such enormous possibilities for loss. No hand but yours can put this great undertaking under way."

I looked at the clock. Close now. I put my finger gently on the red button.

Then I did a double-take and what Doc had said came through to me. I began to swear again. As a European, he had no real notion of the extent, of the minutiae, of the American worship of ignorance. He was traveling on sentiment—

"Mrs. Swain, we are asking that yours be the hand to

launch this adventure. No woman in history has stood at a more momentous crossroads. It may well be that no woman of the future will ever do so much for mankind with so simple a gesture. Would you do us that honor?"

The mike panned to Carol. Her eyes were wide and glassy. I knew she was only in shock, but to the crowd she must have looked petrified with terror. Her mouth moved. She said, "Yes," but no sound came out. All of a sudden the screen went swimming in front of my eyes. I blinked angrily.

Carol fumbled in her survival kit and took out a folder of matches. Doc gave her the signal. She struck a match with trembling fingers and dropped it into the trench.

Nothing happened. The clock ticked toward the first red line.

Another match. Again no result. "Twice, twice," Doc whispered urgently. "Strike them twice!" But she was too far gone to hear. The clock hand passed the first red line.

She struck another one, blindly. I could see Doc frantically searching his own pockets for matches, but he was a nonsmoker—and besides, who brings spare champagne to a launching?

"Fake!" someone in the crowd shouted. The shout was taken up.

The hand went by zero while she was trying to pull still another match free of the folder with her clumsy kitten's paws. Then Doc was trying to take the pack from her, his face twisted with desperation. She hung on with blind tenacity.

The moment of obvious struggle was more than enough for the crowd. It got the first fence down before the marines could even unlimber their rifles. The fence made an uncertain but sufficient bridge across the barbed wire. Carol was still striking matches, but they were, of course, "Hisn" matches, and it would never occur to her to strike them twice. She didn't understand how they worked.

She was still striking matches as the crowd roared up to the launching dugout. I saw Wallingford-Kentworth trying to begin a new speech. Eisenwald was weeping. The crowd-wave broke and frothed over the dugout, a sea of white, staring faces turned toward me.

At the crest of that wave I saw Jim and Dorothy McLaughlin. Salt and soil—and Mr. and Mrs. Peking Man.

The clock hand reached the second red line, and I pushed the button.

The ship-to-ground television showed nothing but a blurred

confusion by the time the rocket took me out of its range at 240 miles up. I don't know how many people were hurt by the initial shock; more than should have been, of that I'm sure. I saw nothing clearly but the faces of Dot and Jim, mouths rounded in O's, eyes wide and glassy, rising after me like implacable balloons.

Now, however, I had myself to think about, and I had to do it in two and a half second tops. I had taken off in time, and could put the ship in her orbit. But nobody would come for me up there, and there I'd die if I insisted on being noble. On the other hand, I couldn't return to America, or I'd likely be torn to pieces—maybe by Jim and Dot, if they were still alive.

I threw the ship high over Baffin Bay, set the controls for a good spectacular crash offshore of Lisbon—the kind of crash that would leave nothing but fused metal—and bailed out. It was easy, as easy as stepping off a ledge.

The passage of the antirocket law is public knowledge. Considering the public's feeling about me—the week-old newspapers that I see up here make it clear that I'm the villain, the man who defied the people and the laws of heaven and injured a lot of just plain folks while I was about it—it isn't safe for me in my own country now.

I wrote to Carol, not directly of course, but through friends in Mexico. Carol ran true to form. She went in the wrong direction. I'm still waiting for my friends to put a forwarding address on her and ship her up here to the camp. It's a long distance between Mexico and Canada, and I don't think she'll like it when she gets here.

Nevertheless. All things considered, the rest of the world, America excluded, can have rocket fever without me.

I'm going to have more than enough excitement as it is, roughing it with Carol.

THE ABATTOIR EFFECT

1

JOAN WREXHAM discovered the Abattoir Effect at four o'clock on a sunny Wednesday afternoon in late June. At the time she was on the fourteenth floor of the Tishman Building, a furiously ugly Manhattan skyscraper which has been described as looking like the box the Seagram Building came in. Its address is also often gives as Sick Sick Sick Fifth Avenue, because it harbors a number of very large and aggressive advertising agencies.

Joan worked for none of them, however; for one thing, she was not pretty enough to risk a client's bumping into her in an agency hallway. She was, instead, peacefully settled in her own office in the suite of the International Blood Rescue Trust, a nonprofit foundation where she had been working for six years. At 4:40, J. Burton Wolverton, director of IBRT, for whom she was supposed to be writing a speech, thrust his prematurely white-haired head into the cubicle.

"Are you getting all the commas in the right places, Joan dear?"

Joan numbly said that she was.

"Good. Make it a dilly, please. Statesmanlike, but with lots of hard sell. We've been having trouble with fund-raising lately . . . sometimes I'm almost sorry we ever discovered that leukemia vaccine. Got to run. See you tomorrow."

He vanished, and though she was fond of him, Joan was glad to see him go. She needed to think, which was virtually impossible in the vicinity of Burton. He worked too hard at being handsome, effusive and dynamic to allow anyone else to concentrate in his presence. For this Joan couldn't blame him. The director of a foundation in the health field depending on the public for funds is in one of the world's most competitive businesses, and if he doesn't keep his public manner polished he soon finds himself director of some less well-heeled foundation. On that road there is only one direction—down.

73

It was this consciousness which had prompted his wryly regretful remark about the leukemia vaccine. Of course IBRT hadn't discovered it. The IBRT maintained no laboratories and had never discovered anything. It merely campaigned for money and then farmed funds out to qualified scientists. But in some ways the Greenberg vaccine had indeed been a disaster for the foundation, which had originally been set up to finance research against just this disease, had paid Greenberg's exceedingly high tabs for years, and had announced his eventual triumph with all the public-relations fanfare at Burton's command. The publicity blasts had aroused some criticism in scientific circles—and had also got Burton in trouble with Washington, where the Commissioner of Health had, as usual, failed to foresee that a vaccine for a disease which mostly attacks children might create a public demand.

Worst of all, however, was that the public, deeming the problem now solved, cut back its annual charity to IBRT by nearly half. But Burton had his answer all ready. Unlike the National Foundation for Infantile Paralysis, he had not waited until the last minute to decide what he was going to do when "his" disease was indeed on the road to being conquered.

In the meantime, quietly, almost stealthily, he had been making himself and IBRT into the transfusion broker for the whole planet.

Not all IBRT's funds went out to scientists; some of them, as was normal, had to be budgeted for administration. In this case, that term covered not only the offices in the Tishman Building, the salaries of Burton and his staff and other overhead items, but IBRT's international register of rare blood types. Every contributor to IBRT had his blood typed free, and unlike Red Cross, the foundation's retained technicians did a most elaborate job of it . . . so elaborate that an IBRT type record was almost as good an identification as a fingerprint. It covered not only "types," defined as something which might affect a transfusion, but "factors," which ordinarily do not; including factors limited to families, circulating antibodies at the time the sample was taken (complete with titers), and half a hundred more recondite items. Immunology can be a more complicated subject than relativity if any real pains is taken with it. All of this was recorded on a punched card, which was given a code number assigned to the donor and written on his IBRT "membership" card, in case of accident.

Accidents or surgery requiring transfusions were not the

only uses to which the IBRT blood-type register was put. There was nothing even vaguely approaching it in scope anywhere else in the world; even the Soviets used it in preference to setting up their own, though whether they would have done so before the *détente* of 1962 was a permanently unanswerable question. It had uses in forensic medicine, all the way from identifying bloodstains involved in crimes to determining, beyond all doubt, cases of disputed parentage. Demographically it was a major index to the immunity levels of whole populations against specific diseases, and hence invaluable to the World Health Organization. It had given the science of human genetics the greatest single impetus since the development of twin studies. And much more.

All this seemed to gratify Burton remotely and impersonally, and he liked to be given the latest statistics and claims to recite in his speeches. But what really counted was that by the time individual donations to IBRT had been cut in half by the Greenberg vaccine, they were being more than made up by consulting fees, library fees, and reprint sales to the UN as an entity and to some seventy of its member governments. The trustees' glowed, and Burton was preserved for another decade from becoming director of the National Fathers' March Against Poison Ivy. Burton had coppered his bets.

It was in the blood-type register—she was consulting it to update the brags in Burton's all-purpose speech—that Joan had discovered the Abattoir Effect: a record, to state the matter with the least paradox the facts allowed, of selective mass murder.

Five o'clock came and went. Joan continued to sit. She had no idea what to do. She had come to New York from Wyoming straight out of college ten years ago, bearing with her a number of convictions of which perhaps the most harmless was that Herbert Hoover had been the last great president of the United States. New York had destroyed most of these quickly and sometimes drastically, but without any particular melodrama. There is, alas, a limit to the amount of trouble a painfully bony, six-foot-two girl can get into in a city full of genuinely beautiful women, no matter how blue her eyes are. Since then she had gone to Europe for three weeks, but had returned with a deepened certainty that although she was for men, they were not for her, at least for more than a few

days. Essentially she still knew nothing about them as a sex,
except that sometimes they couldn't help laughing at her
ignorance. She was, she saw, going to be a spinster—or might
be one already. As for melodrama, well, she *had* run out of
gas on the road to Trieste. Did that count? Probably not.
The future seemed to hold nothing more than endless eve-
nings of warming up canned chow mein in the Village on a
hot plate, and occasional lunches on the expense account,
where she didn't dare take a second martini because it made
her giggle desperately.

And now this. Seeking to vary Burton's almost invariable
text, she had asked Statistics to run a census of how many
Bradbury-immune persons were currently in the blood-type
register. The type was exceedingly rare, and was interesting
because such people often proved also to be abstract reasoners
of the class called "alpha-persistent" by electroencephalog-
raphers. She had encountered the connection in a paper from
a joint EEG-genetics congress held at the Burden Neurological
Institute, published in *Nature*, one of a number of scientific
journals she was expected to read on office time.

There were thirty-four such people in the register. Twenty-
four of them were dead. The age of the oldest deceased was
thirty-one; of the youngest, two. In almost all of the cases
where cause of death was given, it was violent; and Statistics,
when asked to run a one-tailed test on the figures, reported
that p was less than 0.02—meaning that such a distribution
had less than a two per cent likelihood of occurring by chance.

Somebody, or something, was murdering the world's Bradbury-immunes.

Joan had given Statistics the figures without labels; so for
the moment she was the sole proprietor of the knowledge
that "$p < .02$" meant slaughter. It was an unwelcome benison,
and a seemingly useless one. There would be no point in
telling Burton about it; he was no scientist himself, and would
only chuckle at the notion that a frustrated girl on his public
relations staff thought she had made some sort of discovery,
especially one with wild overtones of Eric Ambler. He might
or might not remember that Joan had a degree in physiology,
but if he did he would also recall that she had never worked
in the field after leaving college; he expected and wanted
from her nothing more than "putting the commas in the right
places"—his phrase for writing all his important fund-raising
speeches. Similarly, if he thought about statistics at all, it was
not as a branch of mathematics but as a branch of decorative

lying. He would not recognize a one-tailed test if he met it under a Klieg light. As for Statistics, confronted with a conclusion of this degree of enormity, they would inevitably retreat to saying that the sample wasn't large enough to reach true significance—all very well when it is possible to gather a larger sample, but no help when the sample in question is all the sample attainable for years to come . . . and in the meantime, every new statistic is another murder.

Then again there was a head poking into her cubicle. She nearly jumped. Between the Abattoir Effect and the fact that it was now well after quitting time. . . . But as she might have expected, it was only Deac Winston, the radio and television director, who kept odd hours necessarily.

"Got a comma in the wrong place?" he said.

"Oh, shut up. No, on second thought, come on in if you've got a minute. I need to talk to you."

"If on business, no. Otherwise, yes."

He came on in without waiting for an answer. Deac was a spare man with a stiff crew-cut brush of gray hair and a family of six daughters . . . who had a tendency to punctuate all his continuity with dots . . . like this . . . whom Joan had known ever since her first New York job. If she had a male best friend in town, Deac was it. Certainly he was the only male friend she trusted. And she had abruptly decided that whatever the outcome, this thing had to be confided to somebody.

"I've been hitting Statistics for some figures for Burton, and I think I've found something ugly," she said. "Or maybe it's just a chimera. Whatever it is, promise me you won't laugh."

He listened gravely enough. It astonished her, now that she had committed herself to telling the story aloud, how little there was of it and how slender its factual foundations were. But she plowed on to the end.

"Quite a budget," Deac said when she stopped. "And as you see, I'm not laughing. Now tell me one thing more: is there anything on your unconscious that could account for all this? You know damn well how personal troubles can get reflected back onto the job, especially when the job involves harping all day long on the subject of health. Are you dead sure this isn't simply a case of Interne's Syndrome—something for your analyst, instead of the *cops?*"

"I haven't got an analyst, though God knows I probably need one," Joan said. "But no, Deac, I'm dead sure it isn't.

I've already been through that business of catching every disease I read a clinical paper about. I know better now. There's something here. It's real."

"We'll treat it as such," Deac said promptly, to her inexpressible gratitude. "And I agree with you that there's no point in hitting Burton with it, not yet anyhow. We need a lot more in the way of facts. Is there any pattern to all this?"

"No more than I've told you."

"No, I mean, are these people being killed in any order? Geographical, maybe? Or by age? Or occupation group? If they are, it might even be possible to predict the next victim —and do something about it."

She struck her forehead with the heel of her hand. "I knew I needed you. That never occurred to me—I guess I was feeling a little paralyzed. Let's see, now. Statistics is closed for the night, so we'll have to grapple with it pretty much by inspection. Hmm. Offhand I don't see anything. Do you?"

Deac shook his head. "Nothing in geography or occupation, anyhow. A Czech factory inspector, an Argentinian tradesman, an American poet I never heard of, a Louisiana cotton factor, a minor Egyptian politician—all people of at least a little substance, but after all paupers don't enroll in philanthropic movements. If there's any group that predominates here, it's the American housewife—"

"Which is exactly what you'd expect for a foundation like ours," Joan agreed glumly. "And it isn't a hell of a large plurality. I'm sure Statistics would rule it nonsignificant."

"You know them better than I do, and I'm content to keep it that way," Deac said. "Still it does look as though there's nothing further we can do without their beady little eyes. Let's call a moratorium and go have a drink."

"Okay. I need cheering."

He got up, but suddenly his eyes were arrested by another table of statistics, lying partly concealed by the first on Joan's desk.

"Ulp! What's this? Is this part of it?"

"Well, more or less. Those are our registered Bradbury-immunes that *aren't* dead yet. Just ten of them. But I don't see what good it does us at this point."

"But my God, Joan, look at this. One of these people is Curtis McCormack! What does it matter if he's next on the butchery list, or last? In either case he hasn't far to go—and if they get him there'll be one hell of a stink."

"I can see that, since he's the richest man on the list, but—"

"But nothing. It'll be taken as a political assassination, too. Wars have been caused over less. If you don't know why, I'll explain on the way. Let's hop."

Joan gestured helplessly. "Hop? Where?"

"In a cab, and go see him. What else?"

"But Deac, tonight? He lives in Maine!"

"Tonight. In Maine."

2

They were, in fact, very lucky. In his old age Curtis McCormack was overseas almost constantly, attending conferences and receiving medals and honorary degrees. This was at least in part because he was still nearly as unpopular as ever at home, particularly with the surly patrioteering segments of the U.S. press and public, which had never been able to accept the fact that in the modern world war itself rather than the Soviet Union was the only important enemy. In this they were cheered on by a diminishing band of politicians, Senator Leland in particular, who had been running against Communism for so many years that they had lost all sense of the domestic issues that really mattered to their constituents.

To these people the *détente* of 1962 was the most massive piece of treason since Benedict Arnold, and Curtis McCormack, one of its chief nongovernmental architects, was their most popular whipping boy. They were, furthermore, still strong enough to prevent McCormack's own nation from adequately recognizing his services, though he had been honored everywhere else from Iceland to New Zealand. The fact remained that he had devoted ten extremely active years after his retirement as president of his company to organizing and sponsoring international conferences on nuclear and biological warfare, to getting other peoples' stalled disarmament negotiations on the road again, to publishing and disseminating the results in the teeth of the slave press of one side and the corrupt press of the other sometimes in the teeth of existing security regulations, for which he had twice been convicted and once been sent to jail; the second sentence, suspended, was still hanging over him).

Joan, who was as baffled by politics as she was by men, had known very little of all this. Her total impression of

McCormack up to now had been that he was a senile rich man who had once dabbled in fellow-traveling. For this she was not greatly to be blamed, since half the newspapers that she saw had been striving for a generation to perpetuate just this image of the man. But Deac, who had spent most of his working life before the IBRT job in network news bureaus, had more than enough sophistication to be able to read between the lines . . . and even between the dots.

Consequently he had the good sense to phone McCormack's estate at Portishead before stuffing Joan into the cab and had the great good luck to find that McCormack was not only in the United States, but at home.

"Certainly, I remember you very well," the quavering old voice said. "You gave a very honest account of the second Portishead Conference, for an American reporter. I was impressed."

"Well, sir, this may not be quite as important. But I think it's urgent. Could we possibly come to see you tonight?"

"Why, I could trust your judgment a second time, I believe. Yes. Can you go as far as Newark? Good. Then I'll have my pilot pick you up there."

Deac swallowed audibly. "Thank you, sir. How'll we recognize him?"

"He will probably be there before you arrive. He will have you paged every five minutes. In the meantime, I had better take a nap. Good-bye."

Deac hung up, looking rather dazed, but in a moment he had recovered and was hustling Joan toward the elevators.

"He'll see us?" Joan said incredulously.

"Yes. He's sending his own plane for us. I'll tell you all about it in the cab."

"Uh, Deac, hadn't you better phone your wife?"

"My wife? No need for that. I'm supposed to be sitting up over a hot *Today* show. No hurry to explain it all to her—but it's sure going to take a lot of explaining to Burton. Come *on*, will you? This is *news*—I haven't smelled anything like it in years."

"I am not easily amazed any more," McCormack said. "I have seen too much. But there seems to be no end to the ways technical ingenuity can be enlisted in the service of evil."

He rested his elbow on the arm of his chair and his chin

on his palm, brooding. He was a fragile narrow man, stooped but tall even when seated, with sunken cheeks and bushy white eyebrows. Though impeccably dressed, one could see that his beautiful Shantung suit had been bought some years ago, for it made his wrists and neck look wasted.

"I find I have some questions," he went on at last. "How would anyone know the complete list of . . . Bradbury-immunes? . . . except the experts in your own organization?"

"The register is pretty easy to get to," Joan explained. "Besides the data pool in New York, there are duplicate pools in London, Istanbul, and Tokyo. Often there are emergencies where a doctor wouldn't want to have to wait for a cable from New York—"

"—and they haven't got all the bugs out of satellite-relay radio yet, either," Deac added.

"Yes. And a good many doctors don't feel real confidence in any data analysis they haven't made themselves, and prefer not to use our analysts. So as matters stand now, any licensed physician in the world can have access to our raw data just for the asking."

"I see," McCormack said. "I am grateful to you for taking such pains to warn me. But I don't really see what help I can be to you. This doesn't appear to be a personal vendetta, so there would be no point in my giving you a list of my known enemies—an enormous list it would be, let me assure you. However, show me a man who has no enemies and I will show you a nobody. Nor can I think of anything in particular to do in my own behalf."

There was silence in the great library, except for the distant sough of the storm in the Maine woods outside; it had been a rough flight up, and somehow the open fire was not very heartening. At last Deac said:

"Sir, if I may make a suggestion—"

"Please."

"Wouldn't it be possible to put on a few guards? And perhaps cancel any further trips until we find out what this is all about? We'll get to the bottom of it eventually, I'm sure, but right now . . ."

"Hmm." The old man thought about it, his eyes deeply shadowed. They waited.

"I am as averse to being deprived of my life as any man," McCormack said. "Obviously I'm very old, and can tell myself that I've accomplished many things in my time. But there is always more to do, it is like the stone of Sisyphus, and to some of these tasks I can still put my shoulder. I feel all the more urgent about them because my time is short.

"As for guards, I have them; I have had them for years. I am not going to get in my own way by encumbering myself with an army, however. And I am certainly not going to stop or even curtail my traveling. I think you will understand that for me this would be a form of suicide; that whoever it is that is seeking my death would then have it, whether he knew it or not. Much better for me to go on working and let death take me unwilling, as it would in any case. Not by my own hand, no; not by my own hand."

There was nothing to be said to that. Joan felt her eyes watering; probably the fireplace was smoking a little.

"Has it occurred to either of you that the whole machinery of the blood types may be a piece of misdirection?"

"No, sir," Deac said, startled. "In fact, I'm not even sure I follow you."

"I mean that what may be aimed at here is the death of only one particular person on your list of 34. The fact that he happened to have a rare blood type may have suggested that others with this type be killed to throw the police off, and conceal the real target."

Joan gasped. "This—this Abattoir Effect just for *that*? I can't imagine—"

"You are young," McCormack said tiredly. "You do not remember the death camps. But perhaps that is not the point either; for if a man decides to kill another, he might equally well decide to kill thirty-four. Dylan Thomas said, 'After the first death, there is no other. ' "

"I suppose it's entirely possible," Deac said thoughtfully. "But that brings it right back to you—there's nobody else on the list who's nearly as eminent."

"To the killer?" McCormack said. "He may not be aiming at the best-known target. You know nothing about his reasons. If you did, you would be able to predict his procedure."

"True," Deac admitted. "Then we have a stalemate."

"So it would appear. Let us dismiss it then, and you will be my guests. Obviously you cannot go back to New York now; I will have you flown back in the morning. Tell me, what do you think of the prospects for third-stage disarmament?"

The cab, balked by early morning traffic, dropped them on 52nd Street. They walked arm in arm around the corner, kicking an occasional candy wrapper into the gutter without much improving the scene. They were of course late to work, but happily Burton was not in the office that morning to make a production of forgiving them. There was little else to be happy about; the trip had obviously been fruitless; they knew no more than they had before.

Well, perhaps not entirely fruitless, Joan thought. Meeting McCormack had been a worthwhile experience in itself. She had never before had the sense of being in the presence of greatness, and it had been a little overwhelming. Yet that made the need to stop this slaughter in time all the more urgent.

It did not stop. Bright and early Monday morning, Statistics sent up a memo: Bradbury-immune Heinrich Merck, harpsichord player born in Mainz, killed in a traffic accident in London between sessions of recording all 150 of the Scarlatti sonatas; age, 67; would she please add these data to the records she was holding? And when did she think she might be done with them?

Soon now. There were only nine to go. Shaken and fuming, she beat her way down to Deac's office. He wasn't in; probably he had been sitting up over another night show. There was no point in going back upstairs, for she knew that she would get no work done today; she sat and waited.

He came in only half an hour later, but by that time she was already in a state sufficient to shock him into closing the door at once. "My God, Joan. Unwind. Take it easy. What's the matter?"

She told him. "We've got to stop this," she said, drumming on his desk with the sides of both hands. "We're not doing anything. We've got to *do* something. Right now, right now."

"Sit down," he said firmly, "and shut up. Hysterics will get us no place. Sit *down.*"

She sat, already exhausted, and clenched her hands together.

"Now. I agree. Let's just take it slowly. Okay?"

"But—Okay. I'm sorry."

"That's better. I've been thinking too. But what I've come up with is something you'll have to do all by yourself— I'll be no good to you at all—and you can't do it if you're on a hair trigger. In brief, I think you ought to go to the FBI. They have no jurisdiction over what's going on outside our own country, but they surely are interested in anything that's being plotted against United States citizens, especially including McCormack. The fact that it's country-wide takes it out of the purlieu of the individual states, or at least makes it of possible Federal interest as a conspiracy, rather than a set of individual murders which the states might deal with one by one. And if you *can* convince them that it's also international in scope, they might ring one of the silent services in on it—Counterintelligence, possibly. I just don't know how they divide up the pie. Are you game?"

By now she was quite numb. "Yes. If you think so, Deac. But why just me?"

"Because I'm only a newsman and swing no weight with them. You are the expert."

"All right."

"Let's put it this way. You are not an expert in this kind of thing," the FBI man said with superior kindness. "You've got a little correlation here and it's cute, I have to give you that. But really, you've not a statistician, and you're not an immunologist, and certainly you're not a criminologist. Forgive me, Miss, but we often encounter just this kind of thing: a layman is engaged in a technical job, or in writing about a technical job, and suddenly he assumes that he knows all about the science involved—whereas all he actually can do is sling the jargon, and read it pretty well. But that makes him think he's a scientist. Like, for example, public relations men for drug firms. They practice medicine on their friends and even their families. But that doesn't make them doctors. And finally, if they have a certain cast of mind, they begin to uncover plots."

"You mean you think I'm a paranoid," Joan said.

"I didn't say that. I do say that I'd take more stock in all this if it had come to us from somebody who really knows something about the very complex sciences involved. In your case we reluctantly conclude that you don't. If we had to chase every flying saucer that crossed our doorstep, we'd never catch any real kidnapper or communist. And I ought to remind you also that simple murder is not Federal offense. The rest of the story—well, it's a story. I admit it's a good one. I can't help you any farther than that."

"Won't you—even use a little extra care? I mean in guarding the rest of the people on the list—McCormack and the others?"

"Believe me," the FBI man said with a slow smile, "we never stop watching Mr. McCormack. And some one of these days we're going to get him."

By Friday, the list of survivors was down to eight. Number nine was an American housewife.

Joan was appalled, Deac was merely a little grim. However, he said nothing but, "When are they going to grow up?" As a comment it seemed utterly inadequate, but that description unfortunately fitted all their labors very well.

Joan found it more and more difficult to think about blood, let alone write about it. For the first time in years Burton turned a speech back to her for a rewrite; and from the peeved expression which flitted over his face when he encountered Deac in Joan's office, she gathered that Deac's work was suffering too, relatively hardened against the grimness of the world though he was by his reporter's past. She jumped whenever the phone rang, and was afraid to look at her incoming mail for fear of finding another of those indifferent memos from Statistics.

Thus it was without more than a faint sensation of pleasure heavily overlaid with foreboding that she heard from Deac that McCormack was in town and wanted to see them again. The news, she was sure, could be nothing but bad; and besides, they could neither of them afford to lose more time off the job—

That, at least, did not turn out to be a necessary worry. McCormack had invited them to dinner in his suite at the Waldorf. It was a huge place. Deac called it later "A great place to chase girls in"—even the bathroom was bigger than her whole apartment—and the old man seemed almost lost in its reaches. He paid it no attention; he had been a guest in palaces. Over the brandy, he said:

"Something has happened which puts a slightly different light on our deliberations. As you probably know, I am on my way to the Third Stage Disarmament Conference at Paris. This afternoon I was approached in an implicitly threatening manner by a man unknown to me, who furthermore would not say whom or what he represents. His errand was to 'suggest' to me what my attitude should be toward certain programs to be proposed in Paris. The 'suggestion' is in contradiction to everything I have stood for and fought for since I gave up being a simple-minded company president and went out into the world." He looked very stern; Joan would not care to be the target of that expression.

"Were I to do any part of what he asks, the consequences would be incalculable, especially since I am the secretary-general of the meeting. It is my considered opinion that he represents forces who are seeking to revive the cold war. Of course, I can't accuse any specific parties under the circumstances, but it is not hard to imagine who might belong to such a group."

"You're not going to do it," Deac said. It was not a question.

"That goes without saying. Nevertheless the incident forces me to consider that I am, after all, the single man at whom Miss Wrexham's 'abattoir effect' is aimed, and that the other murders are indeed simply blinds; I am under no other threat of which I have been made aware, nor did my visitor offer any. I offer this in the faint hope that it may somehow change the total picture you are trying to put together, or in some other way serve as a clue—otherwise, I should never have mentioned it at all. It's not the first time I have been threatened."

"I can well imagine," Deac said. "But sir, there's one other aspect that certainly suggests itself here. You wouldn't have been aware of *this* specific threat if Joan and I hadn't brought it to you. This has the nasty effect of implying that we are ourselves a part of the plot."

"Oh, no," Joan said. "Mr. McCormack, we—"

He lifted a freckled, blue-veined hand in a gentle gesture.

"Please. That of course occurred to me. I discarded it. I have not grown so old in this somewhat dangerous career I have carved out without developing an instinct for choosing whom to trust."

"Thank you, sir," Deac said. Joan simply swallowed.

It did not seem to change anything, though they debated it at length the next morning.

"I still can't believe that this—this systematic pogrom is only for misdirection," Joan said. "For one thing, it's world-wide—it has to be, considering the kind of people they're killing off—and that means that whoever's involved has some sort of extensive organization to use. All this couldn't be done by one man, no matter how fast he travels. He'd need time to plan each murder. Every one is a special case, I should think."

"Yes," Deac said. "And inevitably he'd have slipped and gotten caught by now. There's organization involved here, all right, and one hell of a lot of money, too. Another thing: if only one man is the real target, it's only the police in *his* country that would need to be misdirected. Why bother planting a lot of false clues in ten or twenty other countries

—clues they'd more than likely never even hear about? That doesn't make a nickel's worth of sense."

"It was only luck that I happened on them at all," Joan agreed, "and yet IBRT is the most likely place for it to be detected. They were playing for big stakes to take even that much of a chance."

"Which leaves us just where we were before. I swear I'm beginning to feel as though I were responsible for it myself. If we don't get some kind of a break soon I'm going to blow my cork."

"I don't even want to talk about that part of it. But we're missing something, that's very obvious. Let's talk about it just once more a little later. I've got to get this revise to Burton. I don't have the faintest idea what I've made him say this time, and what's more I don't give a damn."

Deac grunted. Three minutes later he grunted again, with astonishment.

"Boy, that was fast."

"It's got to be fast. Listen, Deac, how much do you know about Burton's politics?"

"Why, essentially nothing, I suppose. In public he always sounds pretty far right, but that doesn't mean anything; you can't get money out of most businessmen any other way. You ought to know, you put those things in his mouth."

"Yes, that's it exactly. I have no idea how he really thinks. But when I went up there now, he didn't even look at the speech, though he's been grousing about its being late for days. He was in some kind of very grim conference, and I gather Mary wasn't supposed to let me in there at all. She wasn't at her desk so I just walked in, like always."

"Sure, we all do. In conference with whom?"

"Senator Leland, and a man I only think I recognize. Do you know what John Hoagland looks like?"

Deac whistled. Hoagland was the owner of the Hoagland Syndicate, distinguished for publishing some of the worst newspapers in the world—and the most jingoistic.

"Like the back of my hand. He was my boss for a couple of years. He's a tremendous fellow, with very broad shoulders, about fifty but still with black hair—probably dyed—and a crooked nose he got during the Berlin riots when he was still only a legman. That him?"

"Yes."

"My God. I always knew Burton's taste was lousy, but—Wait a minute. Joan, do you think that *Burton*—"

"Who else?" she said, her mouth like lye. "It all hangs together, like a body from a noose. McCormack was right that we were part of the plot, and he was right that it's aimed at him. They knew they could never scare him by a simple death threat—that's been tried before and never worked. He told us so himself. What they're doing is *killing off all possible donors*. Then they'll stage an 'accident'—something they can be damn sure is going to require a transfusion—and use the IBRT blood bank as blackmail. Healthy, he wouldn't give in to them; dying, they figure maybe he would. If he doesn't, well, at least he's dead, which wouldn't make them sorry either."

Deac looked as sick as she felt. "The lousy—never mind. What can we do? We've got not a shred of proof, let alone being able to stop them."

"We can stop them," Joan said. "If you'll go along with me. It could get us killed too. But it's got to be done."

"I've covered wars in my time," Deac said. "What is it? Spit it out."

Burton was alone when Joan came into his office, quietly closing the door. It was a big place, expensively carpeted and with three windows. On the wall over his head hung a framed document: the Hippocratic Oath.

"Ah, Joan. This is really much better. You are really very good when you've got your mind on your work."

"Thanks," Joan said. She was terrified, but though her legs trembled, her heart was like iron. "I've got news for you, Burton."

"Oh? You had better sit down, dear, you look a little unwell."

"I don't want to sit down, and I'm damn sick. You are going to be sicker pretty soon and maybe even dead. I've just had your personal IBM card in the data pool marked Bradbury-immune."

"What!" He turned white and reached for the phone. Then, as if realizing what the motion might admit, he snatched his hand back.

"Aha. Then you *are* the man."

"I think you'd better go home and see a doctor," Burton said, his voice rasping. "I don't know what you're getting at, but you're obviously in bad shape mentally."

"Too late. You wouldn't have paniced unless you knew what it meant. I've also had cables sent to all the other centers, so the duplicate cards are so marked, too. You can have them pulled, and have me fired, but I've got friends here who will be putting the cards right back in the meantime. Would you like to bet you won't be killed before you can pull them a second time? The Third Stage Disarmament Conference begins next Monday—by that time all the possible donors will have to be dead, or the whole thing goes to waste."

"Supposing," Burton said quietly, "that you and Deac were to have a little accident tonight? I know who your confederate is, of course."

"We are spending the rest of this week with Curtis McCormack, who's very well guarded—as you should know better than anybody else. Deac is with him already, so it wouldn't do any good for me to have an accident on the way over. Incidentally, McCormack knows, too."

Burton drummed on the desk top, his lips a thin bloodless line.

"If you think I can issue any sort of order to stop things," he said, "what's to prevent me from also passing the word that my card is a phony?"

"Nothing. But you can't stop it. Nobody could reach all the killers involved in just four days. If they were that easy to locate, most of them would have been caught by now." This was a guess of Deac's; Joan could only pray silently that it was true. "Besides, do you think Hoagland and the Senator would believe you? Could they afford to take the chance that you're *not* Bradbury-immune, when IBRT's own cards say you are? How long do you think you have to live, Burton?"

"They wouldn't believe it, the bastards," Burton said desperately. He was sweating. "Damn them, I never wanted to get into this thing in the first place. But they had me over a barrel—a little indiscretion many years ago—they *used* me. And now they'll kill me. They would have anyhow. I didn't think of that, but naturally they would, lives are nothing to them—"

Joan took a step forward.

"Burton—why don't you tell?"

"Tell?" he repeated dully. "I'd be—"

"You'd get a lot of years in jail as an accessory. But it's better than letting those two snakes murder you, after all you've done for them. And they'd get the same sentence—or worse."

He licked his lips. "They would," he said. "Oh, they would. With what I know—"

"You'd better hurry, Burton. There's an assassin on your doorstep right now. You know how fast they're working now."

By this time she was standing by his desk, and only a few seconds earlier had managed to press the button summoning Mary. But the door was closed.

Someone knocked.

With a strangled cry, Burton snatched up the phone. "Lock the door, Joan. My God, I'll do it. Don't let anybody in. Hello, hello, this is Mr. Wolverton's office, get me the police, yes yes the police, as fast as you can!"

It was an eternity behind that locked door with Burton—closeted in a skyscraper with a weeping demon. When it was over, the streets of New York looked clean to Joan for the first time in ten years.

THE OATH

REMEMBERING CONSCIENTIOUSLY to use the hand brake as well as the foot. Dr. Frank Tucci began to slow down toward the middle of the bridge, examining the toll booths ahead with a cold eye.

He despised everything about scouting by motor scooter, though he agreed, when forced to it, that a man on a scooter made the smallest possible target consistent with getting anywhere—and besides, it conserved gas, of which there was very little left Most of all he despised crossing bridges. It made him feel even more exposed than usual, and toll booths made natural ambushes.

These, however, were as deserted as they looked. The glass had been broken and the tills rifled. Without question the man who had taken the money had not lived long enough afterward to discover that it was worthless. Still, the looting of money was unusual, for there had been little time for it. Most people outside target areas had died during the first two days; the 38-hour dose in the open had averaged 9100 roentgens.

Naturally the small town ahead would be thoroughly looted of food and other valuables, but that was different. There was a physician in the area—that was the man Dr. Tucci had come all this way to see—and as usual, people would have drifted in again to settle around him. People meant looting, necessarily. For one thing, they were accustomed to getting 70 per cent of their calcium from milk, and the only milk that was drinkable out here was canned stuff from before the Day. There might still be a cow or two alive outside the Vaults, but her milk would be lethal.

There would be no more dairy products of any kind for the lifetime of anyone now living, once the lootables were gone. There was too much strontium-90 in the soil. The Nutrition Board had worked out some way around the calcium supply problem, Tucci had heard, but he knew nothing about it; that wasn't his province.

His province was in the valley ahead, in the large reddish frame house where, all the reports assured him, he would find another doctor—or somebody who was passing for one. The house, he noted professionally, was fairly well situated. There was a broad creek running rapidly over a stone bed not far away, and the land was arable and in cultivation: truck crops for the most part, a good acre of them, enough to supply a small family by today's starvation standards. The family was there, that was evident: two children in the four-to-seven age bracket—hence survivors, both of them—were playing a stalking game in the rows of corn to which the other acre was planted.

Tucci wondered if the owner knew the Indian trick of planting pumpkins, beans, and a fish from the stream in the same hill with the corn. If he didn't, he wasn't getting more than half as much from the acre as he might.

The position was not optimum for defense. Though the centrally located house did offer clear shots all around, anyone could put it under siege almost indefinitely from the high ground which surrounded it. But presumably a doctor did not need to conduct a lonely defense against the rare roving band, since his neighbors would help him. A "neighbor" in that sense would include anyone within a hundred miles who could pick up a weapon and get to the scene fast enough.

Even a mob might pause before it could come to that. Its first sight of the house would be from here, looking down into the valley; and on the roof of the house, over green paint much streaked by repeated antifallout hosings, was painted a large red cross.

That would hardly have protected the owner during the first six months after the Day, but that was more than a year ago. Things had settled somewhat since then. Initially a good deal of venom had expressed itself against doctors when the dying had discovered that they could not be saved. That was why, now, rumors of the existence of a physician could bring Dr. Tucci two hundred bumpy miles on a rusty Lambretta whose side panels had fallen off, carrying a conspicuous five-gallon can of the liquid gold that was gasoline on his luggage rack, sweating inside a bullet-proof suit in whose efficacy he thoroughly disbelieved.

He gunned the motor three times in neutral before putting the scooter back in gear and starting it slowly down the hill. The last thing he wanted was to seem to be sneaking up on anybody. Sure enough, as he clambered down from his perch onto the road in front of the house and lurched the scooter up onto its kickstand, he saw someone watching him from a ground floor window.

He knew that he was an odd sight. Short dumpy men look particularly short and dumpy on motor scooters, and he doubted that his green crash helmet and dark goggles made him look any less bizarre. But those, at least, he could take off. There was nothing he could do right now about the putatively bullet-proof coverall.

He was met at the door by a woman. She was a tall, muscular blonde wearing shorts and a halter, a cloth tying up her hair in the back. He approved of her on sight. She was rather pretty in her own heroic fashion, but more than that, she was obviously strong and active. That was what counted these days, although animal cunning was also very helpful.

"Good morning," he said. He produced from his pocket the ritual gift of canned beans without which it was almost impossible to open negotiations with a stranger. "My name is Frank Tucci, from up north. I'm looking for someone named Gottlieb, Nathan Gottlieb; I think—"

"Thank you, this is where he lives," the woman said, with unusual graciousness. Obviously she was not afraid or suspicious. "I'm Sigrid Gottlieb. You'll have to wait a while, I'm afraid. He's seeing another patient now, and there are several others waiting."

"Patient?" Tucci said, without attempting to look surprised. He knew that he would overdo it. Just speaking slowly should be sufficient for an unsuspicious audience. "But it's—of course everything's different now, but the Gottlieb I'm looking for is a poet."

Another pause. He added, "Er . . . was a poet."

"Is a poet," Sigrid said. "Well, come in please, Mr. Tucci. He'll be astonished. At least, *I'm* astonished—hardly anybody knew his name, even Back Then."

Score one, thanks to the Appalachian Vaults' monstrous library. Out of a personal crotchet, Tucci checked with the library each name that rumor brought him, and this time it had paid off. It never had before.

From here on out, it ought to be easy.

Nathan Gottlieb listened with such intensity that he reduced every other listener in Tucci's memory to little better than a catatonic. His regard made Tucci acutely aware of the several small lies upon which his story rested; and of the fact that Gottlieb was turning over and over in his hands the ritual can of beans Tucci had given Sigrid. In a while, perhaps Gottlieb would see that it had been made *after* the Day, and would draw the appropriate conclusions. Well, there was no help for it. Onward and upward.

Physically, Gottlieb was small and gaunt, nearly a foot shorter than his wife, and rather swarthy. He looked as though, nude, you might be able to count all his bones. His somatotype suggested that he had not looked much plumper Back Then. But the body hardly mattered. What overwhelmed Tucci was the total, balanced alertness which informed its every muscle. Somehow, he kept talking.

". . . Then when the word was brought in that there was not only a settlement here, but that a man named Nathan Gottlieb was some sort of key figure in it, it rang a bell. Sheer accident, since the name was common enough, and I'd never been much of a reader, either; but right away a line came to me and I couldn't get rid of it."

"A line?"

"Yes. It goes: 'And the duned gold clean drifted over the forelock of time.' It had haunted me for years, and when I saw your name in the report, it came back, full force."

"As a last line, it's a smasher," Gottlieb said thoughtfully. "Too bad the rest of the poem wasn't up to it. The trouble was, the minute I thought of it, I knew it was a last line, and I waited around for two years for a poem to come along to go with it. None ever did, so finally I constructed one synthetically, with the predictable bad results."

"Nobody would ever know if you didn't tell them," Tucci said with genuine warmth. He had, as a matter of fact, particularly admired that poem for the two whole days *since* he had first read it. "In any event, I was sufficiently curious to don my parachute-silk underwear and come jolting down here to see if you were the same man as the one who wrote *The Coming-Forth*. I'm delighted to find that you are, but I'm overwhelmed to find you practicing medicine as well! We're terribly short of physicians, and that happens to be my particular department. So all in all it's an incredible coincidence."

"That's for true," Gottlieb said, turning the can around in his hands. "And there's still a part of it that I don't understand. Who is this 'we' you mention?"

"Well. We just call it the Corporation now, since it's the last there is. Originally it was the Bryan Moving and Warehouse Corporation. If you lived in this area Back Then, you may remember our radio commercials on WASM-FM, for our Appalachian Mountain Vaults. 'Businessmen, what would happen to your records if some (unnamed) disaster struck? Put them in our mountain vaults, and die happy.' That was the general pitch."

"I remember. I didn't think you meant it."

"We did. Oddly enough, a good many corporation executives took us at face value, too. When the Day came, of course, it was obvious that those papers were going to be no good to anybody. We threw them out and moved in ourselves, instead. We had thought that would be the most likely outcome and had been planning on it."

Gottlieb nodded, and set the can on the floor between his feet, as though the question it had posed him was now answered. "A sane procedure, that's for sure. Go on."

"Well, since the Reds saturated Washington and the ten 'hard' SAC sites out West, we appear to be the only such major survival project that came through. We've had better than a year to hear differently, and haven't heard a whisper. We know that there were several other industrial projects, but they were conducted in such secrecy that the enemy evidently concluded they were really military. We advertised ours on the radio, and like you, they didn't believe that we could be serious; or so we conclude.

"Now we're out and doing. We're trying to organize a— well, not a government exactly, since we don't want to make laws and we don't want to give orders—but at least the service functions of government, to help bring things into some kind of shape. Doing for people, in short, what they can't do for themselves, especially with things in their present shambles."

"I see. And how do you profit?"

"Profit? In a great many ways, all intangible, but quite real. We attract specialists, which we need. This indebts the community to us and helps us manage it better. It's a large community now, about as big as New York and Pennsylvania combined, though it's shaped rather more like Texas. How many people are included I can't say; we may try to run a census in a year or so. Every specialist we recruit is, so to speak, an argument for reviving the institution of government."

He paused, counted to ten, and added: "I hope you are

persuaded. Now that I've found you out, I'd be most reluctant to let you off the hook."

Gottlieb said, "I'm flattered, but I think you're making a mistake. I'm still only a poet, and as such, quite useless. I'm the world's worst medical man, even in these times."

"Ah. Now that's something I've been burning to ask you. How *did* you get into this profession?"

"Deliberately. When Sigrid and I got alarmed by all those Berlin crises, and then the summit fiasco, and decided to start on a basement shelter out here, I had to start thinking of what I might be able to do if we did survive. There wasn't any way to make a living as a poet Back Then, either, but I'd always been able to turn a marginal dollar as a flack—you know, advertising copy, the trade papers, popular articles, ghosting speeches, all those dodges. But obviously there wasn't going to be anything doing in those lines in a primitive world."

"So you chose medicine instead?" Tucci said. "But why? Surely you had some training in it?"

"Some," Gottlieb said. "I was a medical laboratory technician for four years in World War II—the Army's idea of what to do with a poet, I suppose. I did urinalyses, haemotology, blood chemistry, bacteriology, serology and so on; it involved some ward collecting too, so I got to see the patients, not just their body fluids. At first I did it all by the cookbook, but after a while I began to understand parts of it, and by God I seemed to have a feeling for it. I think most literary people might, if they'd just have been able to get rid of their notion that the humanities were superior to the sciences. You know, the pride of the professor of medieval Latin, really a desperately complicated language, is the fact that he couldn't 'do' simple arithmetic. Hell, *anybody* can do arithmetic; my oldest daughter could 'do' algebra at the age of nine, and I think she's a little retarded. Anyhow, that's why I chose medicine. Nowadays I understand why the real medicos had the interne system Back Then, though. There's nothing that turns you into a doctor like actually working at it, accumulating patient-hours and diagnostic experience."

Tucci nodded abstractedly. "What did you do for equipment, materia medica, and so on?"

"I don't have any equipment to speak of. I don't do even simple surgery; I have to be hyperconservative out of sheer ignorance—lancing a boil and installing a tube drain is as far in that line as I dare to go. And of course I've no electricity. I've been reading up on building a dam across my creek and winding a simple generator, but so far the proposition's been too much for me. I'm not at all handy, though I've been forced to try.

"As for supplies, that was easy—just a matter of knowing in advance what I hoped to do. I simply looted the local drugstore the moment I came out of the hole, while everybody else who'd survived that long was busy loading up on canned goods and clothing and hardware. I was lucky that the whole dodge hadn't occurred to the pharmacist himself before the Day came, but it didn't. He hadn't even thought to dig himself a hole.

"I figured that anything I missed in the line of consumer goods would come my way later, if the doctor business paid off. And you'd be surprised how much of my medical knowledge comes from the package inserts the manufacturers used to include with the drugs. By believing a hundred per cent of the cautions and contraindications, and maybe thirty per cent of the claims, I hardly ever poison a patient."

"Hmmm," Tucci said, suppressing a smile only by a heroic effort. "How long will your supplies hold out?"

"Quite a while yet, I think. I'm being conservative there, too. In infectious cases, for instance, if I have a choice between an antibiotic and a synthetic—such as a sulfa drug— I use the antibiotic, since it has an expiration date and the sulfa drug doesn't. In another year I'm going to have to start doubling my antibiotic doses, but there's no use worrying about that—and I'll still have an ample stock of the synthetics."

Tucci thought about it, conscientiously. It was a strange case, and he was not sure he liked it. Most of the few "doctors" he had tracked down in the field were simple quacks, practicing folk medicine or outright fakery to fill a gap left by the wholesale slaughter of specialists of all kinds, bar none—doctors, plumbers, farmers, you name it, it was almost extinct. Occasionally he had hit a survivor who had been a real physician Back Then; those had been great discoveries, and instantly recruited.

Gottlieb was neither one nor the other. He had no right to practice, by the old educational, lodge-brother or government standards. Yet obviously he was trying to do an honest job from a limited but real base of knowledge. The Vaults could use him, that was certain; but would they offer him the incentives they still reserved for the genuine, 24-carat, pre-Day M.D.?

Tucci decided that they would have to. This was the first case of its kind, but it would not be the last. Sooner or later they would have to face up to it.

"I think we can solve at least some of your problems," he said slowly. "So far as shelf-life of antibiotics is concerned, we keep them in cold storage and have enough to last a good fifty years. We have electricity, and we can give you the use of a great deal of equipment, as you learn how to use it: for example, X-rays, fluoroscopes, ECGs, EEGs. I think we need you, Mr. Gottlieb; and it's self-evident that you need us."

Gottlieb shook his head, slowly, but not at all hesitantly. It took Tucci several seconds to register that that was what he was doing.

"No," he said. "You're very kind. But I'm afraid it doesn't attract me."

The refusal was stunning, but Tucci was well accustomed to shocks. He drew a deep breath and came back fighting.

"For heaven's sake, why not? I don't like to be importunate, but you ought at least to think of what the other advantages might be. You could give up this marginal farming; we have a large enough community so we can leave that to experienced farmers. We use specialists in their specialties. You and your family could live in the Vaults, and breathe filtered air; that alone should run your children's life expectancy up by a decade or more. You know very well that the roentgen level in the open is still far above any trustable level, and if you came out of your hole in anything under three months—as I'm sure you did—you and your family have had your lifetime dose already. And above all, you'd be able to practice medicine in a way that's quite impossible here, and help many more people than you're helping now."

Gottlieb stood up. "I don't doubt a word of that," he said. "The answer is still no. I could explain, but it would be faster in the long run if you first took a look at the kind of medicine I'm actually practicing now. After that the explanations can be shorter, and probably more convincing."

"Well . . . of course. It's your decision. I'll play it your way."

"Good. I've still got three patients out there. I'm aware that you yourself are a bona-fide physician, Dr. Tucci; you disguise it well, but not well enough. And you may not want me so badly when we're through."

The first patient was a burly, bearded, twisted man with heavily calloused hands who might always have been a farmer; in any event, everybody in the field was some kind of farmer now. He stank mightily, and part of the stench seemed to Tucci to be alcohol. His troubles, which he explained surlily, were intimate.

"Before we go on, there's something we have to get clear, Mr. Herwood," Gottlieb told him, in what subsequently proved to be a set speech for new patients. "I'm not a real doctor and I can't promise to help you. I know something about medicine and I'll do the best I can, as I see it. If it doesn't work, you don't pay me. Okay?"

"I don't give a damn," the patient said. "You do what you can, that's okay with me."

"Good." Gottlieb took a smear and rang a little hand bell on his desk. His 15-year-old daughter popped her head in through the swinging door that led to the kitchen, and Gottlieb handed her the slide.

"Check this for gram-positive diplococci," he told her. She nodded and disappeared. Gottlieb filled in the time discussing payment with the patient. Herwood had, it turned out, a small case of anchovy fillets which he had liberated in the first days, when people were grabbing up anything, but nobody in his surviving family would eat them. Only tourists ate such stuff, not people.

The teen-ager pushed open the swinging door again. "Positive," she reported.

"Thanks, honey. Now, Mr. Herwood, who's your contact?"

"Don't follow you."

"Who'd you get this from?"

"I don't have to tell you that."

"Of course you don't," Gottlieb said. "I don't have to treat you, either."

Herwood squirmed in his straight-backed chair. He was obviously in considerable physical discomfort.

"You got no right to blackjack me," he growled. "I thought you was here to help people, not t' make trouble."

"That's right. But I already told you. I'm not a real doctor. I never took the Hippocratic Oath and I'm not *bound* to help anybody. I make up my own mind about that. In this case, I want to see that woman, and if I don't get to see her, I don't treat you."

"Well . . ." Herwood shifted again in the chair. "All right, damn you. You got me over a barrel and you know it. I'll tell her to come in."

"That's only a start," Gottlieb said patiently. "That leaves it up to her. Not good enough. I want to know her name, so if she doesn't show up for treatment here herself, I can do something about it."

"You got no right."

"I said so. But that's how it's going to be."

The argument continued for several minutes more, but it was clear from the beginning that Gottlieb had won it. . . . He gave the man an injection with matter-of-fact skill.

"That should start clearing up the trouble, but don't jump to conclusions when you begin to feel better. It'll be temporary. These things are stubborn. I'll need to see you three more times, at least. So don't forget to tell Gertie that I want to see her—and that I know who she is."

Herwood left, muttering blackly. Gottlieb turned to his observer.

"I see a lot of that kind of thing, of course. I'm doing my best to stamp it out—which I might even be able to do in a population as small and isolated as this," he said. "I don't have any moral strictures on the subject, incidentally. The old codes are gone, and good riddance. In fact, without widespread promiscuity I can't see how we'll ever repopulate the world before we become extinct. But the diseases involved cost us an enormous sum in man-hours; and some of them have long latent periods that store up hell for the next generations. In *this* generation it's actually possible to wipe them out for good and all—and if it can be done, it should be done."

"True," Tucci said noncommitally. Thus far, he was baffled. Gottlieb had done nothing that he would not have done himself.

The next patient was also a man, shockingly plump, though as work-worn as his predecessor. Gottlieb greeted him with obvious affection. His symptoms made up an odd constellation, obviously meaningless to the patient himself; and after a while Tucci began to suspect that they meant very little to Gottlieb, either.

"How did that toe clear up?" Gottlieb was saying.

"All right, fine, Nat. It's just that I keep getting these boils and all every time I hit a splinter, looks like. And lately I'm always thirsty, I can't seem to get enough water; and the more I drink the more it cuts into my sleep, so I'm tired all the time too. The same with food. People are talking, they say I eat like a pig, and it's true, and it shows. But I can't help it. A bad name to have, these days, and me with a family."

"I know what you mean. But it's pretty indefinite now, Hal. We'll just have to wait and see what develops." Gottlieb paused, and quite surreptitiously drew a deep, sad breath. "Try to cut down a little on the intake, I'll give you *some* pills that will help you there, and some sleeping tablets. Don't hit the sleepy pills too hard, though."

Payment was arranged. It was only nominal this time.

"Are you aware," Tucci said when they were alone again, "that you've just committed manslaughter—at the very least?"

"Sure I am," Gottlieb said in a low voice. "I told you you wouldn't like what you saw. The man's a new diabetic. There's nothing I can do for him, that's all."

"Surely that's not so. I'm aware that you can't store insulin without any refrigeration, but surely there were some of the oral hypoglycemic agents in the stock you found at the drugstore—tolbutamide, carbutamide, chlorpropamide? If you don't recognize them by their old trade names, I can help you. In the meantime—well, at least you could have put the man on a rational diet."

"I threw all those pills out," Gottlieb said flatly. "I don't treat diabetics. Period. You heard what I told Herwood: I never took the Hippocratic Oath, and I don't subscribe to it. In the present instance, we're having a hard enough time with all the new antisurvival mutations that have cropped up. I am not going to have any hand in preserving any of the old ones. If I ever hit a hemophiliac, the first thing I'll do is puncture him for a test—and forget to put a patch over the hole. Do you remember, Dr. Tucci, that just before the Day there was a national society soliciting funds to look for a *cure* for hemophilia? When the Oath takes you that far, into saving lethal genes, either it's crazy or you are!"

"What would you have done with LaGuardia? Or Edison?" Tucci said evenly.

"Were they hemophiliacs?" Gottlieb said in astonishment.

"No. But they were diabetics. It's the same thing, in your universe."

After a long time, Gottlieb said, almost to himself:

"I can't say. It isn't easy. Am I to save every lethal gene because I suspect that the man who carries it is a genius? That may have been worth while in the old days, when there were millions of diabetics. But now? The odds are all against it. I make harder decisions than that every day, Dr. Tucci. Hal is no genius, but he's a friend of mine."

"And so you've killed him."

"Yes," Gottlieb said stonily. "He wasn't the first, and he won't be the last. There are not many people left in the world. We cannot tolerate lethal genes. The doctor who does may save one adult life—but he will kill hundreds of children. I won't do that. I never swore to preserve *every* life that was put in my hands, regardless of consequences. That's my curse . . . and my lever on the world."

"In short, you have set yourself up to play God."

"To *play* God?" Gottlieb said. "Now you're talking nonsense. In this village, I *am* God . . . the only god that's left."

The last patient was relatively commonplace. She had frequent, incapacitating headaches—and had earned them, for she had five children, two survivors and three new ones. While Gottlieb doled out aspirin to her (for which he charged a price so stiff—after all, there had been 15,670,944,200 aspirin tablets, approximately, in storage in the United States alone on the Day—that Tucci suspected it was intended to discourage a further visit), Tucci studied her fasciae and certain revealing tics, tremors, and failures of coordination which were more eloquent to him than anything she had said.

"There, that does it for today," Gottlieb said. "And with no more telephones, I'm almost never called out at night—never for anything trivial. I'll clean up and then we can talk further. You'll eat with us, of course. I have a canned Polish ham I've been saving for our first guest after the Day, and you've earned the right to be that guest."

"I'd be honored," Tucci said. "But first, one question. Have you a diagnosis for the last patient?"

"Oh, migraine, I suppose, though that's about as good as no diagnosis at all. Possibly menopausal—or maybe just copelessness. That's a disease I invented, but I see a lot of it. Why?"

"It's not copelessness. It's glioblastoma multiforme—a runaway malignant tumor of the brain. At the moment, that's only a provisional opinion, but I think exploration would confirm it. Aspirin won't last her long—and in the end, neither will morphine."

"Well . . . I'm sorry. Annie's a warm and useful woman. But if you're right, that's that."

"No. We have a treatment. We give the patient a boric acid injection—"

"Great God," Gottlieb said. "The side effects must be fierce."

"Yes, but if the patient is doomed anyhow? . . . After all, it's a little late in the day for gentleness."

"Sorry. Go ahead. Why boric acid?"

"Boron won't ordinarily cross the blood-brain barrier," Tucci explained. "But it will concentrate in the tumor. Then we irradiate the whole brain with slow neutrons. The boron atoms split, emitting two quanta of gamma radiation per atom, and the tumor is destroyed. The fission fragments are nontoxic, and the neutrons don't harm the normal brain tissue. As for the secondary gammas, they can't get through more than a layer of tissue a single cell thick, so they never leave the tumor at all. It works very well—one of our inheritances from Back Then; a man named Lee Farr invented it."

"Fantastic! If only poor Annie could have—" Gottlieb's mouth shut with the suddenness of a rabbit-trap, and his eyes began to narrow.

"Wait a minute," he said. "I'm being a little slow today. You said, 'We *have* a treatment'—not 'We *had*.' What you mean me to understand is that you also have an atomic pile. That's the only possible source of slow neutrons."

"Yes, we have one. It generates our electricity. It's clumsy and inefficient—but we've got it."

"All right," Gottlieb said slowly. "I'll go and change, and then we'll talk. But the purpose of my demonstration, Dr. Tucci, is what I mean *you* to understand; and I wish you'd think about it a while, while I'm gone."

The dinner was enormously pleasant; remarkably good even by the standards of the Vaults, and almost a unique experience in the field. Sigrid Gottlieb proved to be a witty table companion as well as an imaginative cook. Some of her shafts had barbs on them, for it was plain that she had overheard enough to divine Tucci's mission and had chosen to resent it. But these were not frequent enough or jagged enough to make Tucci believe that she was trying to make up her husband's mind for him. All well and good.

As for the children—the one prospect of the meal to which Tucci had not been looking forward, for as a bachelor he was categorically frightened of children—they were not even in evidence. They were fed in the kitchen by the eldest, the same girl who served as her father's laboratory technician.

There was no medical talk until dinner was over. Instead, Gottlieb talked of poetry, with a curious mixture of intensity and wistfulness. This kept his guest a little on guard. Tucci knew more than most surviving Americans about the subject, he was sure, but far less than he had pretended to know.

Afterward, however, Gottlieb got directly to the point. "Any conclusions?" he said.

"A few," Tucci said, refusing to be rushed. "I'm still quite convinced that you'd be better off with us. I'm not terribly alarmed by your odd brand of medicine—and I don't know whether you were afraid I would be, or whether you meant me to be. In the Vaults, we sometimes have to short-circuit the Oath too, for similar reasons."

"Yes. I don't doubt that you do. The Oath was full of traps even Back Then," Gottlieb said. "But I hoped you'd see that there's more to my refusal to join you than that. To begin with, Dr. Tucci, *I don't like medicine;* so I don't care whether I could do it better in the Vaults, or not."

"Oh? Well, then, you're quite right. I have somehow missed the point."

"It's this. You say you are so well organized that you can use specialists as specialists, rather than requiring them to do their own subsistence farming, policing, and so on. But—could you use me *as a poet*? No, of course not. I'd have to practice medicine in the Vaults.

"But to what end? I really hate medicine. No, I shouldn't say that, but I'm certainly no fonder of it than I am of farming. I picked it as a profession because I knew it would be in demand after the Day—and that's all.

"In your Vaults I'd be an apprentice, to a trade I don't much like. After all, you're sure to have real MDs there, beginning with yourself. All of a sudden, I'd be nobody. And more than that, I'd lose control over policy—over the kind of medicine *I* think suitable for the world we live in now—which is the only aspect of my practice that does interest me. I don't want to save diabetics at your behest. I want to let them die, at mine. Call it playing God if you like, but nothing else makes sense to me now. Do you follow me?"

"I'm afraid I do. But go on anyhow."

"There isn't much farther to go. I'm satisfied where I am—that's the essence of it. My patients may not be as well served by me as they think they are, but all the same they swear by me and come back for more. And I'm the only one of my kind in these parts. I don't have to farm my place to the last square inch because most of my fees are in kind—which is lucky, because I have a brown thumb. Sigrid is a little better with plants, but not much. I don't have to fortify it, or keep a twenty-four hour watch, because my patients wouldn't dare let anything happen to me. I don't need the medical facilities, the laboratories and equipment and so on that you're offering me, because I wouldn't know how to use them.

"So of course I'll keep on the way I've been going. What else could I do?"

"I'm sure," Tucci said quietly, "that you'd find plenty of time in the Vaults to practice poetry as well—and many people who value it. I doubt that you find either here."

"What of it? Poetry has been a private art for a century, anyhow," Gottlieb said bitterly. "Certainly it's no art for a captive audience, which wants to pat the poet on the head because it thinks he's really valuable for something quite different, like writing advertising copy or practicing medicine. I'm no longer interested in being tolerated. I wrote that off the day before the Day, and I'm not going back to it."

"But surely if—"

"Listen to me, Dr. Tucci," Gottlieb said. "If you are really running a sort of Institute for Advanced Study, and can promise me *all* my time to perfect myself as a poet, I'll go with you."

"Obviously, I can't make such a promise."

"Then I'll stay here. If I *have* to practice medicine, I may as well do so under conditions that I myself have laid down. Otherwise it would be too unrewarding for me to even tolerate. I wasn't really called to the vocation in the beginning, and there are times even now when it makes me quite sick. I can't help it; that's the way I am."

"So we have nothing more to say to each other, it seems," Tucci said. "I'm truly sorry that it worked out this way. I had no idea that the question would even arise. But, in a way, I'm on your side. And besides, were you to come with us, you'd leave your own people without a doctor—and though many of them would doubtless follow you into our community, there must be almost as many who wouldn't be able to do so."

"That's true," Gottlieb said, but he said it with a sort of convulsive shrug, as of a man who would dismiss the question and finds that it is not so easy as that. "Thank you anyhow for the offer. I must say that I feel a little like a boy getting a diploma; all this fakery, and now . . . well; and it's run so late that you will have to spend the night with us. I don't want the Vaults to lose you on my account."

"I'm grateful for all your thoughtfulness—yours, and your wife's as well."

"Come back when you can," Gottlieb said, "and we'll talk poetry some more."

"Thank you," Tucci said inadequately. And that was all. He was guided up to bed, in the wake of a hurricane lamp.

Or was it all? In the insect-strident night, so full of reminders of how many birds had died after the Day, and how loaded with insensible latent death was the black air he breathed as he lay tense in the big cool bed, Tucci was visited by a whole procession of phantoms. Mostly they were images of himself. Some of them were dismissable as nightmares, surfacing during brief shallow naps from which he was awakened by convulsive starts that made his whole body leap against the sheets, as though his muscles were crazily trying to relax in a single bound the moment sleep freed them from the tensions of his cortex. He was used to that. It had been going on for years, and he had come to take it as a sign that though he was not yet deeply asleep, he would be shortly. In the meantime, the nightmares were fantastic and entertaining, not at all like the smothering, dread-loaded replays of the Day which woke him groaning and drenched with sweat many mornings just after dawn.

This time the starts did not presage deep sleep; instead, they left him wide awake and considering images of himself more disquieting than any he could remember having seen in dreams. One of the shallow nightmares was a fantasy of what might be going on in the Gottlieb's bedroom—evidently Sigrid had marked Tucci's celibate psyche more profoundly than he had realized—but from this he awoke suddenly to find himself staring at the invisible ceiling and straining to visualize, not the passages of love between the poet and his wife about which he had been dreaming, but what they might be saying about Dr. Frank Tucci and his errand.

That errand hadn't looked hard to begin with. By all the rules of this kind of operation, Sigrid should now be bringing all possible feminine pressures to bear against Gottlieb's stand, and furthermore, she should be winning. After all, she would think first of her children, an argument of almost absolute potency compared with Gottlieb's abstract and selfish reasons for refusing to go to the Vaults. That was generally how it went.

But Gottlieb was not typical. He was, in fact, decidedly hard upon Tucci's image of himself. He was a quack, by his own admission, but he was not a charlatan—a distinction without a difference before the Day, but presently one of the highest importance, now that Tucci was forced to think about it. And in this cool darkness after the preliminary, complacent nightmares, Tucci was beginning to see himself with horror as a flipped coin. Not a quack, no. He was an authentic doctor with a pre-Day degree, nobody could take that away from him. But he *was* a charlatan, or at the very least a shill. When, after all, had Tucci last practiced medicine? Not since the Day. Ever since, he had been scooting about the empty menacingly quiet countryside on recruiting errands—practicing trickery, not medicine.

Outside, a cloud rolled off the moon, and somewhere nearby a chorus of spring peepers began to sing: *Here we are, here we are, here we are. . . .* They had been tadpoles in the mud when the hot water had come down toward the rivers in the spring floods; they might be bearing heavy radiation loads, but that was not something they were equipped to think about. They were celebrating only the eternal *now* in which they had become inch-long frogs, each with a St. Andrew's cross upon its back . . . *Here we are, we made it . . .*

Here we are. We made it. Some are quacks, and nevertheless practice medicine as best they can. Some are flacks, for all their qualifications, and do nothing but shill . . . and burden the practitioners with hard decisions the Tuccis have become adroit at ducking. The Tuccis can always say that they were specialists before the Day—Tucci himself had been an electrophysiologist, and most of the machines that he needed to continue down the road were still unavailable in the Vaults—but every doctor *begins* as a general practitioner. Was there any excuse, now, for shilling instead of practicing?

The phantoms marched whitely across the ceiling. Their answer was *No*, and again. *No*.

In this world, in fact, Gottlieb was a doctor, and Dr. Frank Tucci was not. That was the last nightmare of all.

He was ruminatively strapping his gear onto the baggage rack of the scooter, very early the next morning, when he heard the screen door bang and looked up to see Gottlieb coming down the front walk toward him. There were, he saw for the first time, tall lilacs and lilies of the valley blooming all around the sides of the house. It was hard to believe that the world had ended, even here in Gottlieb's hollow. He straightened painfully in the bullet-proof suit and hoisted his bubble goggles.

"Nice of you," he said. "But you really needn't have seen me off. Keeping doctor's hours, you need all the sleep you can store up."

"Oh sure," Gottlieb said abstractedly. He leaned on the sagging gate. "But I wanted to talk to you. I had some trouble sleeping—I was thinking—I woke up this morning on the floor, and that hasn't happened to me since just before my final exams. If you've got a minute—"

"Of course. Certainly. But I'd like to get on the road before too long, to skip some of the heat of the day. This helmet absolutely fries my brains when the sun is high."

"Sure. I only wanted to say—I've changed my mind."

"Well. *That* was worth waiing for." Tucci took the helmet off and dropped the goggles carefully into it. "I hope you won't mind if I'm in a hurry, or rather, if *we're* in a hurry. We'll have trucks down here for you in about a week at the latest; it takes a while to get a convoy organized. We'll also send a bus, since I think you'll find that about half your patients will want to follow you, once you've explained the proposition to them."

"That'll cost a lot of gasoline," Gottlieb said. He seemed embarrassed and disturbed.

Tucci waited a moment, and then said, very gently: "If you don't mind, Mr. Gottlieb, would you tell me why you reversed yourself? I'd about given up."

"It's my own fault," Gottlieb broke out, in a transport of anger. "I must have given that speech about the Hippocratic Oath two thousand times in the last year or so. I never took the Oath, that's a fact, and I don't believe in it. But . . . you said I'd be able to treat more patients, and treat them better, if I went to work for you. That's been on my mind all night. And I can't get away from it. It began to look to me as though a man can't be just half a doctor, whether that's all he wants or not. And I did go into this doctor business by my own choice."

He scuffed at the foot of the gate with one broganed toe, as though he might kick it if no one were watching him.

"So there I am. I have to go with you—and never mind that I'm giving up everything I've won so far—and a lot more that I hoped for. I may stop hating you five or ten years from now. But I could have spared myself, if I hadn't been so superior about Hippocrates all this time and just minded my own business."

"The oath that you don't take," Tucci agreed, resuming his goggles and helmet, "is often more binding than the one you do."

He stamped on the kick starter. Miraculously, the battered old Lambretta spat and began to snarl on the first try. Gottlieb stepped back, with a gesture of farewell. At the last moment, however, something else seemed to occur to him.

"Dr. Tucci!" he shouted above the noise of the one-lung engine.

"Yes? Better make it loud, Mr. Gottlieb—I'm almost deaf aboard this thing."

"It's not 'the forelock of time,' you know," Gottlieb said. He did not seem to be yelling, but Tucci could hear him quite plainly. "The word in the poem is 'forepaws.'"

Tucci nodded gravely, glad that the helmet and goggles could be counted on to mask his expression, and put the scooter in gear. As he tooled off up the hill, his methodical mind began to chew slowly, gently, inexorably upon the question of who had been manipulating whom.

He knew that it would be a good many years before he had an answer.

"I'VE GOT definite proof that we've been granted a reprieve," Lord Rogge was insisting to thin air. "Perfectly definite proof."

We had been listening, either tensely or with resignation, according to the man, to the evening news roundup in the bar of the Orchid Club. With the world tottering on the brink, you might have thought that an announcement like that would have elicited at least some interest. Had Rogge said the same thing in public, the reporters would have spread it to the antipodes in half an hour.

Which only goes to show that the world knew less than it should about poor old George. Once the Orchid Club got to know him intimately, it had become impossible to believe in him any longer as one of the world's wise men. Oh, he is one of the great mathematicians of all time, to be sure, but on any other subject he can be counted on to make a complete ass of himself. Most of us already knew, in a general way, what he meant by a "reprieve," and how well his proof would stand up—supported, as usual, by a pillar of ectoplasm.

"What is it now, George?" I said. Somebody has to draw him off, or he'll continue to clamor for attention through the news bulletins. It was now my turn.

"It's proof," he said, sitting down beside me at once. "I've found a marvelous woman in Soho—oh, a perfect illiterate, she has no idea of the magnitude of the thing she's got hold of. But Charles, she has a pipeline to the gods, as clear and direct a contact as any human being ever had. I've written proof of it."

"And the gods tell her that truth and light will prevail? George, don't you *ever* listen to the wireless? Don't you know that these are almost surely our last days? Don't you know that your medium is never going to have another child, that the earth's last generation has already been born, that the final war is upon us right at this instant?"

"Bother," Rogge said, exactly as he might have spoken

had he found soda instead of water in his whisky. "You can't
see beyond the end of your nose, Charles. Here you are, a
speck in a finite universe in finite time, full of *Angst* because
there may not be any more specks. What does that matter?
You're a member of a finite class. If you ever thought about
it all, you knew from the beginning that the class was doomed
to be finite. What do you care about its ultimate cardinality?"

". . . has accused India of deliberately attempting to wreck
the conference," the wireless was saying. "Meanwhile, the
new government of Kashmir which seized power last week
has signed a treaty of 'everlasting friendship and assistance'
with the Peiping government. The latest reports still do not
reveal . . ."

Well, I'd be briefed later; that was part of the agreement.
I said, "I thought you were the one who cared about cardinality. Wouldn't you like to see the number of the class
of human beings get up some day into your precious transfinite realm? How can we do that if we kill each other off this
very month?"

"We can't do it in any case, not in the physical sense,"
Rogge said, settling back into his chair. "No matter how long
the race lives or how fruitful it is, it will always be denumer-
able—each member of the race can be put in one-to-one rela-
tionship with the integers. If we all lived forever and produced
descendants at a great rate, we might wind up as a denumerably infinite class—in infinite time. But we haven't got
infinite time; and in any case, the very first transfinite number
is the cardinal number of *all* such classes. No, my boy, we'll
never make it."

I was, to say the least, irritated. How the man could be so
smug in the face of the red ruin staring us all in the face . . .

"So the reprieve you were talking about is no reprieve for
us."

"It may well be, but that's the smallest part of the implica-
tions. . . . Have you another of those panatelas, Charles? . . .
There now. No, what I was talking about was a reprieve for
the universe. It's been given a chance to live up to man."

"You really ought to listen to the B.B.C. for a few minutes,"
I said. "Just to get some idea of what man is. Not much for
the universe to live up to."

"But it's a two-penny universe to begin with," Rogge said,
from behind a cloud of newborn smoke. "There's no scope
to it. It's certainly no more than ten billion years old at the

outside, and already it's dying. The space-time bubble may or may not continue to expand forever, but before long there won't be anything in it worth noticing. It's ridiculously finite."

"So is man."

"Granted, Charles, but man has already made that heritage look stupid. We've thought of things that utterly transcend the universe we live in."

"Numbers, I suppose."

"Numbers indeed," Rogge said, unruffled. "Transfinite numbers. Numbers larger than infinity. And we live in a universe where they don't appear to stand for anything. A piece of primer-work, like confining a grown man in a pram."

I looked back at the wireless. "We don't sound so grown-up to me."

"Oh, you're not grown-up, Charles, and that holds true for most people. But a few men have shown what the race could do. Look at Cantor. He thought his way right out of the universe he lived in. He created a realm of numbers which evolve logically out of the numbers the universe runs on—and then found no provision had been made for them in the universe as it stands. Which would seem to indicate that Whoever created this universe knew less math than Cantor did! Isn't that silly?"

"I've no opinion," I said. "But you're a religious man, George. Aren't you skirting blasphemy?"

"Don't talk nonsense. Obviously there was a mathematician involved somewhere, and there are no bad mathematicians. If this one was as good as His handiwork indicates, of course He knew about the transfinites; the limitation was purposeful. And I think I've found out the purpose."

Now, of course, the great revelation was due. Promptly on schedule, Rogge fussed inside his jacket pocket. I sat back and waited. He finally produced a grubby piece of paper, a fragment of a kraft bag.

"You're going to need a little background here," he said, drawing the paper out of reach as I leaned forward again. "Transfinite numbers don't work like finite ones. They don't add, subtract, multiply, or divide in any normal sense. As a matter of fact, the only way to change one is to involute it—to raise it to its own power."

"I'm bored already," I said.

"No doubt, but you'll listen because you have to." He grinned at me through the cigar smoke, and I began to feel rather uncomfortable. Could the old boy have been tipped off to our rotating system of running interference with him? "But I'll try to make it clear. Suppose that all the ordinary numbers you know were to change their behavior, so that zero to the zero power, instead of making zero, made one? Then one to the first power would make two; two squared would equal three; three cubed would be four, and so on. Any other operation would leave you just where you were: two times three, for instance, would equal three, and ten times 63 would equal 63. If your ordinary numbers behaved that way, you'd probably be considerably confused at first, but you'd get used to it.

"Well, that's the way the transfinite numbers work. The first one is Aleph-null, which as I said before is the cardinal number of all denumerably infinite classes. If you multiply it by itself, you get Aleph-one. Aleph-one to the Aleph-first equals Aleph-two. Do you follow me?"

"Reluctantly. Now let me crack *your* brains for a minute. What do these numbers number?"

Rogge smiled more gently. "Numbers," he said. "You'll have to try harder than that, Charles."

"You said Aleph-null was the cardinal number of—of all the countably infinite classes, isn't that right? All right, then what is Aleph-one the cardinal number of?"

"Of the class of all real numbers. It's sometimes called C, or the power of the continuum. Unhappily, the continuum as we know it seems to have no use for it."

"And Aleph-two?"

"Is the cardinal number of the class of all one-valued functions."

"Very good." I had been watching this process with considerable secret glee. Rogge is sometimes pitifully easy to trap, I had been told, if you've read his works and know his preoccupations; and I'd taken the trouble to do so. "It seems to me that you've blasted your own argument. First you say that these transfinite numbers don't stand for anything in the real universe. Then you proceed to tell me, one by one, what they stand for."

Rogge looked stunned for an instant, and I got ready to go back to listening to the wireless. But I had misinterpreted his expression. I hadn't stumped him; he had simply underestimated my ignorance, one of his more ingratiating failings.

"But Charles," he said, "to be sure the transfinite numbers stand for numbers. The point is that *they stand for nothing else*. We can apply a finite number, such as seven, to the universe; we can, perhaps, point to seven apples. But there aren't Aleph-one apples in the universe; there aren't Aleph-one atoms in the universe; there is no distance in the universe as great as Aleph-one miles; and the universe won't last for Aleph-one years. The number Aleph-one applies only to concepts of number, which are things existing solely in the minds of men. Why, Charles, we don't even know if there is such a thing as infinity in nature. Or we didn't know until now. At this present moment, not even infinity exists."

Impossibly enough, Rogge was actually beginning to make me feel a little bit circumscribed, a little bit offended that the universe was so paltry. I looked around. Cyril Weaver was sitting closest to the broadcaster, and there were tears running down his craggy face onto his medals. John Boyd was pacing, slamming his fist repeatedly and mechanically into his left palm. Off in the corner next to the fire, Sir Leslie Crawford was well along into one of his ghastly silent drunks, which wind up in a fixed, cataleptic glare at some inconsequential object, such as a tuft in the carpet or the space where a waiter once stood; he was Her Majesty's Undersecretary for Air, but at such moments no event or appeal can reach him.

Evidently nothing that had come through on the wireless had redeemed our expectations in the slightest. Of them all, I was the only one—not counting Lord Rogge, of course—who had failed to hear the news, and so would still be listening for a word of hope during tomorrow's broadcast.

"Almost thou persuadest me, George," I said. "But I warn you, none of this affects my opinion of mediums and spiritualism in the least. So your cause is lost in advance."

"My boy, I'm not going to ask you to believe anything but what I'm going to put before your own eyes. This charwoman, as I said, is utterly uneducated. She happens to have a great gift, but not the slightest idea of how to use it. She stages seances for ignorant folk like herself, and gives out written messages which purport to be from her clientele's departed relatives. The usual thing."

"Not at all impressive as a start."

"No, but wait," Rogge said. "I'm interested in such things, as you know, and I got wind of her through the Psychical Research Society. It seems that some of the woman's patrons had been complaining. They couldn't understand the spirit messages. 'Uncle Bill, 'e wasn't never no one to talk like that.' That sort of complaint. I wouldn't have bothered at all, if I hadn't seen one of the 'messages,' and after that I couldn't wait to see her.

"She was terrified, as such people are of anybody who speaks reasonable English and asks questions. I won't rehearse the details, but eventually she admitted that she's been practicing a fraud on her trade."

"Remarkable."

"I agree," Rogge said, somewhat mockingly, it seemed to me. "It appears that the voices she hears during her trances are *not* the voices of the relatives of her neighbors. As a matter of fact, she isn't even sure that they're spirit voices, or human voices. And she doesn't herself understand what it is that they say. She just writes it down, and then, once she's conscious again, tries to twist what she's written enough to make it apply to the particular client."

I expect I had begun to look a little sour. Rogge held up a hand as if to forestall an interruption. "After I got her calmed down sufficiently, I had her do the trick for me. Believe me, I'm not easily fooled after all these years. That trance was genuine enough, and the writing was fully automatic. I performed several tests to make sure. And this is what she wrote."

Without any attempt at a dramatic pause, he passed the scrap of brown paper over to me. The block printing on it was coarse, sprawling, and badly formed; it had evidently been written with a soft pencil, and there were smudge marks to show where the heel of a hand had rested. The text read:

FYI WER XTENDIN THE FIE NIGHT CONTIN YOU UMBRELLAS OF THIS CROWN ON TO OMEGA AHED OF SHEDYULE DO TO CHRIST IS IN HEAVEN ROOSHIAN OF CHILDREN OPEN SUDO SPEAR TO POSITIV CURVACHER AND BEGIN TRANSFORMATION TO COZ MOST OF MACRO SCOPICK NUMBER

I handed the paper back to Rogge, astonished to find that my heart had sunk. I hadn't realized that it had attained any altitude from which to sink. Had I really been expecting some sort of heavenly pardon through this absurd channel? But I suppose that, in this last agony of the world, anyone might have grasped at the same straw.

"On to omega, indeed," I said. "But don't forget your bumbershoot. How did she manage to spell 'transformation' right?"

"She wears one," Rogge said. "And that's the key to the whole thing. Obviously she didn't understand more than a few words of what she—well, what she overheard. So she tried to convert it into familiar terms, letting a lot of umbrellas and Russians into it in the process. If you read the message phonetically, though, you can spot the interpolations easily— and converted back into its own terms, it's perhaps the most important message anybody on earth ever got."

"If anybody told me that message was from Uncle Bill, I wouldn't just guess it was a fraud. Go ahead, translate."

"First of all, it's obviously a memorandum of some sort. FYI—for your information. The rest says: 'We are extending the finite continuum as of this chronon to omega ahead of schedule due to crisis in evolution of children. Open pseudo-sphere to positive curvature and begin transformation to cosmos of macroscopic number.' "

"Well," I said, "it's certainly more resonant that way. But just as empty."

"By no means. Consider, Charles. Omega is the cardinal number of infinity. The finite continuum is our universe. A chronon can be nothing but a unit of time, probably the basic Pythagorean time-point. The pseudosphere is the shape our universe maintains in four-dimensional space-time. To open it to a positive curvature would, in effect, change it from finite to infinite."

I took time out to relight my cigar and try to apply the glossary to the message. To my consternation, it worked. I got the cheroot back into action only a second before my hands began to shake.

"My word, George," I said, carefully. "Some creature with a spiral nebula for a head has taken up reading your books."

He said nothing, he simply looked at me. At last I had to ask him the preposterous question which I could not drive from me in any other way.

"George," I said, "George, are we the children?"

"I don't know," Rogge said frankly. "I came here convinced that we are. But while talking to you I began to wonder again. Whatever powers sent and received this message evidently regard *some* race in this universe as their children, to be educated gradually into their world—a world where transfinite numbers are everyday facts of arithmetic, and finite numbers are just infinitesimal curiosities. Those powers are graduating that race to an infinite universe as the first step in the change.

"The human race has learned about transfinite numbers, which would seem to be a crucial stage in such an education.

And we're certainly in the midst of a crisis in our evolution. We seem to qualify. But . . . Well, there are quite a few planets in this universe, Charles. We may be the children of whom they speak. Or they may not even know that we exist!"

He got up, his face troubled. "The gods," he said quietly. "They're out there, somewhere in a realm beyond infinity, getting ready to open up our pseudospherical egg and spill us out into an inconceivably vaster universe. But is it for our benefit or for—someone else's? And how will we detect it when it happens? On what time-scale do they plan to do it— tomorrow for us, or tomorrow for them, billions of years too late for us?"

"Or," I said, "the whole thing may be a phantom."

"It may be," he said. He knew, I think, that I had said that for the record, but he gave no sign of it. "Well, in the meantime you're relieved of duty, Charles. I shan't keep you any longer. I had to tell someone, and I have. Think about it."

He went out, his chin ducked reflectively, dribbling cigar ashes onto his vest.

I thought about it. It was, of course, the sheerest nonsense. The woman's scrawled "message" was gibberish. Where Lord Rogge had read into it the mathematical terms with which he was most familiar, someone else might read into it the jargon of some other specialty. How else could a charwoman speak the language of relativity and transfinite numbers? Of course, she might have been picking some expert's brains by telepathy, maybe even Rogge's own—but that explanation just substituted one miracle for another. If I was going to believe in telepathy, I might as well admit that I'd just read an interoffice memo from Olympus.

The Third Programme had gone back to music now, but there was another sound in the bar. It was not very loud, but steady and pervasive. It could be felt in the floor, even through the thick-piled carpet, and it shook the air slightly. Sir Leslie's gaze stirred from the vase upon which it had finally become fixed, and rose slowly, slowly toward the dark oak ceiling. There was a preliminary flicker from the lights.

Children of the gods—

We would know soon now. The bombers were coming.

THE MASKS

THE GIRL'S FACE was quite expression-
less, with a rigidity which might have been either defiance
or fear. She had her hands folded oddly in her lap.

"Lay your hands upon the table," the interrogator said.
"We're aware that they're painted."

He seemed totally bored as he talked. Perhaps there had
been a time when his display of knowledge had been intended
to make prisoners feel that everything was already known,
but now he did not seem to be taking even that much interest
in his job.

"You are Margret Noland, address dormitory 458, north
arm, Bethesda T, Washington," he said. "Husband's name
Lincoln Noland. No work permit. Number, 26, L24, 10x5."

"Is that what it is?" she said. "I can never remember."

The interrogator wrote something down; probably it was
Reactionary, resists duodecimal number system. But all he
said was, "Lay your hands upon the table," in exactly the
same tone of voice.

Margret obeyed this time. Her fingernails were minutely
and elaborately colored, each with a different design. It had
recently become a common fashion, though hardly in the
swarming unemployed of the dormitories. The girl was not
wearing the wrist-charm magnifying lens used by upper-class
women—that is, women with rooms and jobs of their own—
to examine each other's new nail tattoos.

"You make these," the interrogator said.

"No, I don't," Margret said. "I—just apply them."

"Without a work permit."

"Yes," she said, in a whisper.

"How?"

"They call me," she said. "I go to them."

"We know that. How do you apply them?"

"Well, first I give the nails a base coat to fill up the ridges
in the nails," she said hesitantly. "It's very smooth when it
dries, and sensitive to light. Then I put a mask over the nail,

118

ike a negative. Ordinary fluorescent light is enough for the
xposure. Developing them is harder, to bring up the colors
roperly; all you need is water and a little iodine, but the
emperatures have to be just right."

Her voice had gradually begun to take on a tinge of
desperate eagerness, as though against all sanity she thought
he interrogator's interest might be merely technical. Suddenly, however, she seemed to remember once more where
he was.

"It's—easy," she said. "Like washing a child's hands. Not
ke work at all."

"You have never had children," the interrogator said
rutally. "Who supplies the masks?"

"Different people," she said, expressionless once more. "I
et them here and there. People sell them; it's legal."

The interrogator touched a switch. Her hands were bathed
a warm light. On a screen to his left, the ten pathetically
arish fingernails appeared in full color, considerably enlarged.

" 'They call me. I go to them,' " he said, without any real
ttempt to mimic her. "And then someone calls us. You are
a demand; your designs are original, imaginative—and reac-
ionary. Now, what is that?"

His own index finger appeared on the screen opposite one
f hers. "What's that?"

"It's a—I don't know just what it is. Something very ancient.
A design on a shield, from back when they had shields. I
on't know any more."

"You don't know what the writing on the scroll says?"

"I—I didn't know it was writing. It's just curlicues."

" 'Polloi andres os eis aner,' " the interrogator read. "You
on't know what that means?"

"No, please, I didn't know it said anything at all."

"Not even if it kills you?"

"No. No. Please, it's only a design, only a design."

His finger shifted suddenly on the table and on the screen.
And what is that?"

"That's nothing at all," she said, sounding a little surer
f her ground. "Just tiny colored dots in a random pattern.
People like to look at them and imagine shapes in them—
omething like looking at clouds."

There was a muted click and the warm light changed to
pure cadmium red; at the same time, the single fingernail
illed most of the screen. In the monochromatic light the

design no longer had color of its own, but dot-formed letters were now plainly visible.

GUNS DUE
5/11 PASS
WORD

"We have those guns," the interrogator said. "And most of the 'many men as one man,' as well. Now, once more: who supplies the masks?"

"All right," Margret said. "I make them. Without a work permit."

"You have just committed suicide. Are you fully aware of that?"

She tried to shrug. "It's dreadful to be alive without a job. I don't care."

"Your husband is a skilled microengraver."

"He has a work permit," she said.

"Limited. It doesn't cover him as a designer."

She was silent. Slowly, she removed her hands from the table and folded them again in upon themselves, nails to palms, like a child playing "Here's the church and here's the steeple." The interrogator watched, and for the first time his face showed a flicker of interest.

"So," he said. "The game is over, but you are still hiding the clues. Your husband probably is hiding by now. You had better tell me the rest very rapidly."

There was no answer.

"If we need to run all the necessary tests," the interrogator said with a certain avid gentleness, "we will have to remove the nails. If you are helpful, we *might* give you an anesthetic first."

Suddenly the girl seemed to wilt. She leaned forward and put her closed fist on the table, thumb up.

"It's a map," she said dully. "Ultraviolet brings it out. It's a little dim, but please go slowly—it burns me if it becomes very bright."

Without comment, the interrogator snapped a switch. This time there was no visible light, but all the same the UV came pouring down at full intensity, so that in a split second the girl's wrist and arm began to sunburn angrily. Yet on the screen appeared no pattern at all—only an almost invisibly fast flickering of greenish light.

The interrogator sat bolt upright with a terrible, ringing

cry of despair. A sudden convulsion threw him to the floor.

The thumbnail gave up its last thin coating of fluorescent paint with a burst of light from the screen. Margret withdrew her arm, which was already beginning to blister, and walked around the table. The interrogator sprawled silent, motionless. Linc had been right, the man was an epileptoid; a few seconds of flicker-feedback had brought on a full-scale *grand mal* seizure.

There was, of course, no way out—not after that scream. The room would be filled with guards any minute. But they had the interrogator now. He would have no memory of what had happened to him, and it could be made to happen again and again, until his superiors became alarmed enough to replace him. That would not be for a while, for it might take years to begin to suspect that his "accidents" were epileptic. This one, for instance, was going to look like violence; she drew back her foot and kicked him precisely under one ear.

The sharp burning pain in her foream made it hard for her to kick gently enough, but somehow she managed it.

There was a blurred shouting in the corridor outside. She looked around. It had all been done and she could hope for no more. She peeled the mask off her other thumb and swallowed it.

The poison was very fast. She had time only to remember once more that applying the masks had been absurdly like washing a child's hands.

TESTAMENT OF ANDROS

Beside the hearth lie the ashes. There are voices in them. Listen:

MY NAME is Theodor Andresson. I will write my story if you wish. I was at one time resident in astrophysics at Krajputnii, which I may safely describe as the greatest center of learning in the Middle East, perhaps of the entire Eastern Hemisphere. Later—until the chain of incidents which brought me to this *Zucht-Haus*—I was professor emeritus in radioastronomy at Calimyrna University, where I did the work leading to the discovery of the solar pulsation cycle.

I am sure that this work is not credited to me; that is of no importance. I would like it clearly understood that I am not making this record for your benefit, but for mine. Your request means nothing to me, and your pretense of interest in what I may write cannot deceive me. My erstwhile colleagues in the so-called sciences were masters of this kind of pretense. But they, too, were unable to prevent me from penetrating the masquerade at the end. How then does a simple doctor hope to succeed where the finest charlatanry has failed?

And what is allocation of credit—of what importance is priority of discovery before the inexorability of the pulsation cycle? It will work to its new conclusion without regard for your beliefs, my colleagues', or mine. Neither the pretended solicitude nor the real metal bars with which you have surrounded me will matter after that.

I proceed, therefore, to the matter at hand. My position at Calimyrna in that remote time before the cycle was discovered befited my age (eighty-four years) and the reputation I had achieved in my specialty. I was in excellent health, though subject occasionally to depressions of spirit, readily ascribable to my being in a still-strange land and to those scars inflicted upon me in earlier times.

Despite these fits of moodiness, I had every reason to be happy. My eminence in my field afforded me the utmost satisfaction. Despite poverty and persecution in youth, I had won through to security. I had married Marguerita L——, in her youth and mine the toast of twelve continents, not only for her beauty but for her voice. I can still hear now the sound of her singing as I heard it for the first time—singing, on the stage of La Scala in Moscow, the rapturous quartet from the second act of Wagner's *Tristan et Messalina*.

It is quite true—I admit it immediately and calmly—that there were certain flaws in my world, even at Calimyrna. I do not mean the distractions which in old age replace, in the ordinary man, the furies of youth, but rather certain faults and fissures which I found in the world outside myself.

Even a man of my attainments expects at some time to grow old, and to find that process changing the way in which he looks at the world around him. There comes a time, however, when even the most rational of men dust notice when these changes exceed the bounds of reason, when they begin to become extraordinary, even sinister. Shall I be specific? Consider, then—quite calmly—the fact that Marguerita did not herself grow old.

I passed into my eighth decade without taking more than perfunctory notice. I was deeply involved in the solar work we were then carrying on at Calimyrna. I had with me a young graduate student, a brilliant fellow of about thirty, who assisted me and who made certain original contributions of his own to the study. His name, and you will recognize it, was Mario di Ferruci. Calimyrna had completed its thousand-inch radiotelescope, the largest such antenna anywhere in the world, except for the 250-foot Manchester instrument. This was at once put to work in the search for so-called radio stars—those invisible bodies, many of them doubtless nearer to Earth than the nearest visible star, which can be detected only by their emission in the radio spectrum.

Completion of the thousand-inch freed the 600-inch paraboloid antenna for my use in solar work. The smaller instrument had insufficient beam width between half-power points for the critical stellar studies, but it was more suitable for my purpose.

I had in mind at that time a study of the disturbed sun. Hagen of the Naval Research Laboratory had already done the definitive study on the sun in its quiet state. I found myself more drawn to what goes on in the inferno of the sunspots—in the enormous, puzzling catastrophes of the solar flares—the ejection of immense radioactive clouds from the sun's interior high into its atmosphere.

It had already become clear that the radio-frequency emission from the disturbed sun was not, and could not be, thermal in origin, as is the RF emission of the quiet sun. The equivalent temperature of the disturbed sun in selected regions at times rises to billions of degrees, rendering the whole concept of thermal equivalency meaningless.

That the problem was not merely academic impressed me from the first. I have, if you will allow me the term, always had a sense of destiny, of *Schicksal*, an almost Spenglerian awareness of the pressure of fate against the retaining walls of human survival. It is not unique in me; I lay it to my Teutonic ancestry. And when I first encountered the problem of the disturbed sun, something within me felt that I had found destiny itself.

For here, just *here*, was the problem in which destiny was interested, in which some fateful answer awaited the asking of the omnipotent question. I felt this from the moment I first opened Hagen's famous paper—NRL Report 3504—and the more deeply I became interested in the sun as an RF radiator, the more the sensation grew.

Yet how to describe it? I was eighty-four, and this was early in 1956. In all those preceding years I had not known that the mortal frame could sustain such an emotion. Shall I call it a sensation of enormous, unresolvable dread? But I felt at the same time an ecstasy beyond joy, beyond love, beyond belief. And these transports of rapture and terror did not alternate as do the moods of an insane man, but occurred simultaneously—they were one and the same emotion.

Nor did the solar flares prove themselves unworthy of such deep responses. Flares have been observed in many stars. Some of them have been major outbursts, as indeed they would have to be to be visible to us at all. That such a flare could never occur on our own sun, furthermore, could not be said with certainty, for flares are local phenomena—they expend their energy only on one side of a star, not in all directions like a nova—and we had already seen the great detonation of July 29, 1948, on our own sun, which reached an energy level one hundred times the output of the quiet sun, which showed that we did not dare to set limits to what our own sun might yet do.

It was here, however, that I ran into trouble with young di Ferruci. He persistently and stubbornly refused to accept the analogy.

"It's penny-dreadful," he would say, as he had said dozens of times before. "You remind me of Dr. Richardson's stories —you know, the ones he writes for those magazines, about the sun going nova and all that. Whenever it's cloudy at Palomar he dreams up a new catastrophe."

"Richardson is no fool," I would point out. "Other suns have exploded. If he wants to postulate that it could happen to ours, he has every right to do so."

"Sure, Dr. Andresson, in a story," di Ferruci would object. "But as a serious proposition it doesn't hold water. Our sun just isn't the spectral type that goes nova; it hasn't ever even approached the critical instability percentage. It can't even produce a good flare of the Beta Centauri type."

"I don't expect it to go nova. But it's quite capable of producing a major flare, in my opinion. I expect to prove it."

Di Ferruci would shrug, as he always did. "I wouldn't ride any money on you, Dr. Andresson. But I'll be more than interested in what the telescope shows. Let's see what we have here right now. The thermocouple's been calibrated; shall I cut in the hot load?"

At this point—I am now reporting a particular incident, although it, too, was typical of many of these conversations— I became aware that Marguerita was in the observatory. I swung sharply around, considerably annoyed. My wife is innocent of astronomical knowledge, and her usually ill-timed obtrusions upon our routine—although I suppose they were born of the desire to "take an interest" in her husband's profession—were distracting.

Today, however, I was not only annoyed, but stunned. How had I failed to notice this before—I, who pride myself on the acuity of my observation? What stood before me was a young woman!

How shall I say how young? These things are relative. We had married when she was thirty-six and I was forty-four. A difference of eight years is virtually no difference during the middle decades, though it is enormous when both parties are young. Marguerita had been in no sense a child at the time of our marriage.

Yet now, as I was finding, a spread as small as eight years can again become enormous when the dividing line of old age insensibly approaches. And the difference was even greater than this, for now Marguerita, as she stood looking down at our day's three-dimensional graph of solar activity, seemed no older to me than on the day I had first met her; a woman tall, graceful, lithe, platinum-haired, and with the somber, smoldering, unreadable face of Eve—and yet, compared to me now, a child in truth.

"Good afternoon, Mrs. Andresson," di Ferruci said, smiling.

She looked up and smiled back. "Good afternoon," she said. "I see you're about to take another series of readings. Don't let me interrupt you."

"That's quite all right; thus far it's routine," di Ferruci said. I glanced sidewise at him and then back to my wife. "We'd just begun to take readings to break up the monotony of the old argument."

"That's true," I said. "But it would be just as well if you didn't drop in on us unexpectedly, Marguerita. If this had been a critical stage—"

"I'm sorry," she said contritely. "I should have phoned, but I'm always afraid that the telephone will interrupt you, too. When I'm here I can hope to see whether or not you're busy—and you can see who's calling. The telephone has no eyes."

She touched the graph delicately. This graph, I should explain, is made of fourteen curves cut out in cardboard, and assembled so that one set of seven curved pieces is at right angles to the other set. It expresses the variation in intensity of RF emanation across the surface of the sun at the ten-centimeter wave length, where our readings commonly are taken; we make a new such model each day. It shows at a glance, by valley or peak, any deviation from the sun's normal output, thus helping us greatly in interpreting our results.

"How strange it looks today," she said. "It's always in motion, like a comber racing toward the shore. I keep expecting it to begin to break at the top."

Di Ferruci stopped tinkering with the drive clock and sat down before the control desk, his blue-black helmet of hair—only a little peppered by his memories of the Inchon landing—swiveling sharply toward her. I could not see his face. "What an eerie notion," he said. "Mrs. Andresson, you and the doctor'll have me sharing your presentiments of doom any minute now."

"It isn't a question of presentiments," I said sharply. "You should be aware by now, Mario, that in the RF range the sun is a variable star. Does that mean nothing to you? Let me ask you another question. How do you explain Eta Carina?"

"What's Eta Carina?" Marguerita said.

I did not know quite how to begin answering her, but di Ferruci, who lacked my intimate knowledge of her limitations, had no such qualms.

"It's a freak—one of the worst freaks of the past ten years," he said eagerly. "It's a star that's gone nova three times. The last time was in 1952, about a hundred years before the previous explosion. Before that it had an outburst in the 1600s, and it may have blown up about 142 A.D., too. Each time it gains in brightness nearly one hundred thousand times—as violent a stellar catastrophe as you can find anywhere in the records." He offered the data to her like a bouquet, and before I could begin to take offense, swung back upon me again. "Surely, Doc, you don't maintain that Eta Carina is a flare star?"

"All stars are flare stars," I said, looking steadily at him. His eyes were in shadow. "More than that: all stars are novas, in the long run. Young stars like our sun are variable only in the radio spectrum, but gradually they become more and more unstable, and begin to produce small flares. Then come the big flares, like the Beta Centauri outburst; then they go nova; and then the cycle begins again."

"Evidence?"

"Everywhere. The process goes on in little in the short-term variables, the Cepheids. Eta Carina shows how it works in a smaller, noncluster star. The other novas we've observed simply have longer periods—they haven't had time to go nova again within recorded history. *But they will.*"

"Well," di Ferruci said, "if that's so, Richardson's visions of our sun exploding seem almost pleasant. You see us being roasted gradually instead, in a series of hotter and hotter flares. When does the first one hit us, by your figures?"

Mario was watching me steadily. Perhaps I looked strange, for I was once again in the grip of that anomalous emotion, so impossible to describe, in which terror and ecstasy blended and fused into some whole beyond any possibility of communication. As I stated for the first time what I saw, and saw so clearly, was ahead for us all, this deep radical emotion began to shake me as if I had stepped all unawares from the comfortable island of relative, weighable facts into some blastingly cold ocean of Absolute Truth.

"I don't know," I said. "It needs checking. But I give us six months."

Marguerita's and di Ferruci's eyes met. Then he said, "Let's check it then. We should be able to find the instability threshold for each stage, from RR Lyrae stars right through classical Cepheids, long-periods, and irregulars to radio-variables. We already know the figure for novas. Let's dot the i's and cross the t's—and then find out where our sun stands."

"Theodor," Marguerita said, "what—what will happen if you're right?"

"Then the next flare will be immensely greater than the 1948 one. The Earth will survive it; life on Earth probably will not, certainly not human life."

Marguerita remained standing beside the model a moment longer, nursing the hand which had been touching it. Then she looked at me out of eyes too young for me to read, and left the observatory.

With a hasty word to di Ferruci, I followed her, berating myself as I went. Suspecting as I did the shortness of the span left to us, I had planned not to utter a word about what was in store in her presence; that was one of the reasons why I had objected to her visits to the observatory. There had simply been no reason to cloud our last months together with the shadow of a fate she could not understand.

But when I reached the top of the granite steps leading down to the road, she was gone—nor could I see either her figure or any sign of a car on the road which led down the mountain. She had vanished as completely as if she had never existed.

Needless to say, I was disturbed. There are cabins in the woods, only a short distance from the observatory proper, which are used by staff members as temporary residences. We had never made use of them—radioastronomy being an art which can be carried on by day better than by night—but nevertheless I checked them systematically. It was inconceivable to me that she could be in the main observatory, but I searched that too, as well as the solar tower and the Schmidt shed.

She was nowhere. By the time I had finished searching, it was sunset and there was no longer any use in returning to my own instrument. I could only conclude that I had miscalculated the time lag between her exit and my pursuit, and that I would find her at home.

Yet somehow I did not go home. All during my search of

the grounds another thought had been in my head! What if I was wrong? Suppose there was no solar pulsation cycle? Suppose my figures were meaningless? If this seems to be a strange thing for a man to be thinking, while searching for an inexplicably vanished wife, I can only say that the two subjects seemed to me to be somehow not unconnected.

And as it turned out, I was right. I have said that I have a sense of fate.

In the end, I went back to the observatory, now dark and, I supposed, deserted. But there was a light glowing softly inside, the evenly lit surface of the transparency viewer. Bent over it, his features floating eerily in nothingness, was Mario di Ferruci.

I groped for the switch, found it, and the fluorescents flashed on overhead. Mario straightened, blinking.

"Mario, what are you doing here? I thought you had left before sundown."

"I meant to," di Ferruci said slowly. "But I couldn't stop thinking about your theory. It isn't every day that one hears the end of the world announced by a man of your eminence. I decided I just had to run my own check, or else go nuts wondering."

"Why couldn't you have waited for me?" I said. "We could have done the work together much quicker and more easily."

"That's true," he said slowly. "But, Dr. Andresson, I'm just a graduate student, and you're a famous man, young as you are. I'm a little afraid of being overwhelmed—of missing an error because you've checked it already, or failing to check some point at all—that kind of thing. After all, we're all going to die if you're right, and that's hardly a minor matter. So I thought I'd try paddling my own canoe. Maybe I'll find the world just as far up the creek as you do. But I had to try."

It took me a while to digest this, distracted as I already was. After a while I said, as calmly as I could: "And what have you found?"

"Dr. Andresson—*you're wrong.*"

For an instant I could not see. All the red raw exploding universe of unstable stars went wheeling through my old head like maddened atoms. But I am a scientist. I conquered it.

"Wherein am I wrong?"

Di Ferruci took a deep breath. His face was white and set

under the fluorescents. "Dr. Andresson, forgive me; this is a hard thing for me to say. But the error in your calcs is way the hell back in the beginning, in your thermodynamic assumptions. It lies in the step between the Chapman-Cowling expression, and your derivation for the coefficient of mutual diffusion. Your derivation is perfectly sound in classical thermodynamics, but that isn't what we have to deal with here. We're dealing instead with a completely ionized binary gas, where your quantity D 12 becomes nothing more than a first approximation."

"I never called it anything else."

"Maybe not," di Ferruci said doggedly. "But your math handles it as an absolute. By the time your expanded equation fifty-eight is reached, you've lost a complete set of subscripts and your expressions for the electron of charge wind up all as odd powers! I'm not impugning your logic—it's fantastically brilliant—but insofar as it derives from the bracketed expression D 12 it doesn't represent a real situation."

He stared at me, half-defiantly, half in a kind of anxiety the source of which I could not fathom. It had been many years since I was young; now I was gravid with death—his, mine, yours, Marguerita's, everyone's. I said only: "Let's check it again."

But we never had the chance; at that moment the door opened soundlessly, and Marguerita came back.

"Theodor, Mario!" she said breathlessly. "Are you trying to work yourselves to death? Let's all live to our appointed times, whenever they come! Theodor, I was so frightened when you didn't come home—why didn't you call—"

"I'm not sure anyone would have answered," I said grimly. "Or if someone had, I would have suspected her of being an impostor—or a teleport."

She turned her strange look upon me. "I—don't understand you."

"I hope you don't, Marguerita. We'll take that matter up in private. Right now we're making a check. Dr. di Ferruci was about to knock the solar pulsation theory to flinders when you entered."

"Doc!" di Ferruci protested. "That wasn't the point at all. I just wanted to find—"

"Don't call me 'Doc'!"

"Very well," di Ferruci said. His face became whiter still. "But I insist on finishing my sentence. I'm not out to kick apart your theory; I think it's a brilliant theory and that it may still very well be right. There are holes in your math, that's all. They're big holes and they need filling; maybe, between us we could fill them. But if you don't care enough to want to do the job, why should I?"

"Why, indeed?"

He stared at me with fury for a moment. Then he put his hand distractedly to his forehead, stood up slowly, and began to pace. "Look, Doc—Dr. Andresson. Believe me, I'm not hostile to the idea. It scares me, but that's only because I'm human. There's still a good chance that it's basically sound. If we could go to work on it now, really intensively, we might be able to have it in shape for the triple-A-S meeting in Chicago two months from now. It'd set every physicist, every astronomer, every scientist of any stripe on his ear!"

And there was the clue for which, all unconsciously, I had been waiting. "Indeed it would," I said. "And for four months, old Dr. Andresson and young Dr. Ferruci would be famous, as perhaps no scientists had ever been famous before. Old Dr. Andresson has had his measure of fame and has lost his faith in it. But for young Dr. Ferruci, even four months would be a deep draft. For that he is willing to impugn his senior's work, to force endless conferences, to call everything into question—all to get his own name added to the credits on the final paper."

"Theodor," Marguerita said. "Theodor, this isn't like you. If—"

"And there is even a touch of humor in this little playlet," I said. "The old man would have credited young Dr. Ferruci in the final paper in any case. The whole maneuver was for nothing."

"There was no maneuver," di Ferruci ground out, his fists clenched. The nervous movements of his hand across his forehead had turned his blue-black hair into a mare's nest. "I'm not an idiot. I know that if you're right, the whole world will be in ashes before the year is out—including any research papers which might carry my name, and any human eyes which might see them.

"What I want to do is to pin down this concept to the point where it's unassailable. The world will demand nothing less of it than that. *Then* it can be presented to the AAAS— and the world will have four months during which the best scientific brains on Earth can look for an out, a way to save at least a part of the race, even if only two people. What's fame to me, or anyone else, if this theory is right?

Gas, just gas. But if we can make the world believe it, utterly and completely, then the world will find a loophole. Nothing less than the combined brains of the whole of science could do the job—and we won't get those brains to work unless we convince them!"

"Nonsense," I said calmly. "There is no 'out,' as you put it. But I'll agree that I looked deeper into you than I needed for a motive. Do you think that I have overlooked all these odd coincidences? Here is my wife, and here are you, both at improbable hours, neither of you expecting me; here is young Dr. di Ferruci interrupted at his task of stealing something more than just my work; here is Marguerita Andresson, emerged from wherever she has been hiding all evening, unable to believe that Earth's last picture is all but painted, but ready to help a young man with blue-black hair to steal the pretty notion and capitalize on it."

There was a faint sound from Marguerita. I did not look at her.

After a long while, di Ferruci said: "You are a great astronomer, Dr. Andresson. I owe you twenty years of inspiration from a distance, and five years of the finest training a master ever gave a tyro.

"You are also foul-minded, cruel-tongued, and very much mistaken. I resign from this University as of now; my obligation to you is wiped out by what you saw fit to say of me." He searched for his jacket, failed to find it, and gave up at once in trembling fury. "Good-bye, Mrs. Andresson, with my deepest sympathy. And Doc, good-bye—and God have mercy on you."

"Wait," I said. I moved then, after what seemed a century of standing frozen. The young man stopped, his hand halfway to the doorknob, and his back to me. Watching him, I found my way to a chart-viewer, and picked up the pair of six-inch dividers he had been using to check my charts.

"Well?" he said.

"It's not so easy as that, Mario. You don't walk out of a house with the stolen goods under your arm when the owner is present. A strong man armed keepeth his house. You may not leave. You may not take my hard-won theory to another university. You may not leave Hamelin with pipes in your hand. You may not carry both my heart and my brains out of this observatory as easily as you would carry a sack of potatoes. In short—*you may not leave!*"

I threw the points of the dividers high and launched myelf soul and body at that hunched, broad back. Marguerta's sudden scream rang deafeningly as a siren in the observatory dome.

The rest you know.

I have been honest with you. Tell me, where have you idden her now?

1. I, Andrew, a servant of the Sun, who also am your rother, he who was called and was sanctified, say unto you, lessed be he that readeth, and keepeth the word; for behold, he time is at hand; be thou content.

2. For behold, it was given to me, in the City of Angels, pon a high hill, to look upon His face; whereupon I fell own and wept.

3. And He said, I am the Be-All and End-All; I am the Being and the Becoming; except that they be pure, none shall ook upon Me else they die, for the time is at hand. And when He had spoken thus, I was sore afraid.

4. And He said, Rise up, and go forth unto the peoples, and say thou, Unless thou repent, I will come to thee quickly, and shine My countenance upon thee. I shall loosen the seals, and sound the trumpets, and open the vials, and the deaths which shall come upon thee will be numbered as seven times even.

5. The Sun shall become black as sackcloth of hair, and the moon become as blood; and the stars of heaven shall fall onto the earth, and the heaven depart as a scroll when it is rolled together, and every mountain and island be moved out of its place. And all men shall hide themselves and say to the mountains and rocks, Fall on us, and hide us from the face of Him that sitteth on the throne.

6. There will be hail and fire mingled with blood, and these cast upon the earth; a great mountain burning with fire shall be cast into the sea; and there will fall a great star from heaven, burning as it were a lamp, upon the fountains of waters; and the third part of the Sun shall be smitten, and the third part of the moon; and there shall arise a smoke out of the pit, so that the air and the day be darkened.

7. And if there be any who worship not Me, and who heed not, I say unto you all, woe, woe, for ye shall all die; ye shall feast without sacraments, ye shall batten upon each other; ye shall be clouds without water, driven by dry winds; ye shall be dry sterile trees, twice dead, and withered; wander-

ing stars, to whom is given the dark of the emptiness of
eternity; verily, I say unto you:

8. Ye shall be tormented with fire and brimstone, the third
part of trees shall be burnt up, and all green grass be burnt
up, and the third part of creatures which were in the sea,
and had life, shall die; and the waters shall become blood,
and many men die of the waters, because they be bitter; and
ever, and thou shalt have no rest, neither day nor night; for
the hour of judgment is come.

9. And saying thus, He that spake to me departed, and
His dread spirit, and I went down among the people, and
spoke, and bade men beware; and none heeded.

10. Neither those who worshiped the stars, and consulted,
one among the others; nor those who worshiped man and his
image; nor those who made prayers to the invisible spirits of
the air; nor those who worshiped any other thing; and the
spirit of Him who had spoken was heavy upon me, so I
went unto my chambers and lay me down in a swound.

11. And the angel of the Sun spoke to me as I lay, and
spake with a voice like trombones, and said, Behold, all
men are evil, but thou shalt redeem them, albeit thou remain a pure child of the Sun, and thou alone. Thou shalt
have power; a two-edged sword shall go out of thy mouth,
and thou shalt hold seven times seven stars in thy palm, and
be puissant; this I shall give thee as thine own, if only thou
remainest, and thou alone. And I said: Lord, I am Thine;
do with me as Thou wilt.

12. And I went forth again, and spoke, and the nations
of men harkened, and the kings of the world bent the knee,
and the princes of the world brought tribute, seven times
seven; and those who worshiped the stars, and the spirits
of the air, and all other things, bowed down before Him;
and it was well with them.

13. Now at this time there appeared a great wonder in
heaven: a star clothed in a glory of hair, like a woman; and
the people gathered and murmured of wonder, saying, Beware, for there is a god in the sky, clothed in hair like a
woman, and with streaming of robes and bright garments;
and, behold, it draws near in the night, and fears not the
Sun; and the hem of this robe gathers about us.

14. And there arose a woman of the world, and came forward, preaching the gospel of the wild star, saying: Our
god the Sun is a false god; his mate is this great star; they
will devour us. There is no god but man.

15. And this woman, which was called Margo, summoned the people and made laughter with them, and derision, and scorned the Sun, and gave herself to the priests of the voices in the air, and to those who worshiped numbers, and to the kings and princes of the world; and there was whirling of tambourines in the high towers of the Sun.

16. And the angel of the Sun spoke to me with the sound of trombones, saying, Go with thy power which had been given to thee, and crush this woman, else thou shalt be given to the wild star, and to the flames of the wild star's hair, and with thee the world; I command thee, slay this woman, for thou hast been given the power, nor shall it be given thee again; I have spoken.

17. And I went, and the woman called Margo spoke unto me, saying: Thou art fair, and hath power. Give me of thy power, and I will give you of mine. Neither the wild star nor the Sun shall have such power as we have.

18. And I looked upon her, and she was fair, beyond all the daughters of the earth; and when she spoke, her voice was as the sounding of bells; and there was a spirit in her greater than the souls of men; and a star, clothed in a glory of hair, with streaming of robes and bright garments; and I kissed the hem of her robe.

19. And the voice of the angel of the Sun was heard like a sounding of trombones, saying: Thou hast yielded thy power to an harlot, and given the earth to the fire; thy power is riven from thee, and all shall die;

20. So be it.

My name is George Anders. I have no hope that anyone will read this record, which will probably be destroyed with me—I have no safer place to put it than on my person—but I write it anyhow, if only to show that man was a talkative animal to his last gasp. If the day of glory which has been foretold comes about, there may well be a new and better world which will cherish what I put down here—but I am desperately afraid that the terrible here-and-now is the day the voices promised, and that there will be nothing else for ever and ever.

This is not to say that the voices lied. But since that first night when they spoke to me, I have come to know that they speak for forces of tremendous power, forces to which human life is as nothing. A day of glory we have already had, truly—but such a day as no man could long for.

It was on the morning of March 18 that that day dawned, with a sun so huge as to dominate the entire eastern sky, a flaring monster which made the memory of our accustomed sun seem like a match flame. All the previous night had been as hot as high summer, although not four days before we had a blizzard. Now, with the rising of this colossal globe, we learned the real meaning of heat.

A day of glory, of glory incredible—and deadly. The heat grew and grew. By a little after noon the temperature in the shade was more than one hundred fifty degrees, and in the open—it is impossible to describe what an inferno it was under the direct rays of that sun. A bucket of water thrown into the street from a window boiled in midair before it could strike the pavement.

In some parts of the city, where there were wooden buildings and asphalt or tarred-black streets, everything was burning. In the country, the radio said, it was worse; forests were ablaze, grasslands, wheatfields, everything. Curiously, it was this that saved many of us, for before the afternoon could reach its full fury the sky was gray with smoke, cutting off at least a little of the rays of that solar horror. Flakes of ash fell everywhere.

Millions died that day. Only a few in refrigerated rooms—meat-coolers, cold-storage warehouses, the blast-tunnels for frozen-food firms, underground fur-storage vaults—survived, where the refrigeration apparatus itself survived. By a little after midnight, the outside temperature had dropped only to slightly above one hundred degrees, and the trembling and half-mad wraiths who still lived emerged to look silently at the ruined world.

I was one of these. I had planned that I would be. Months before, I had known that this day of doom was to come upon us, for the voices had said so. I can still remember—for as long as I live I will remember, whether it be a day or forty years—the onset of that strange feeling, that withdrawal from the world around me, as if everything familiar had suddenly become as unreal as a stage-setting. What had seemed commonplace became strange, sinister. What was that man doing with the bottles which contained the white fluid? Why was the uniform he wore also white? Why not blood in the bottles? And the man with the huge assemblage of paper; why was he watching it so intently as he sat in the subway? Did he expect it to make some sudden move if he looked away? Were the black marks with which the paper was covered the footprints of some minuscule horde?

And as the world underwent its slow transformation, the voices came. I cannot write here what they said, because paper would not bear such words. But the meaning was clear. The destruction of the world was at hand. And beyond it—

Beyond it, the day of glory. A turn toward something new, something before which all men's previous knowledge of grandeur would pale. A new Apocalypse and Resurrection? So it seemed, then. But the voices spoke in symbol and parable, and perhaps the rising of the hellish sun was the only "day of glory" we would ever see.

And so I hid in my shelter, and survived that day. When I first emerged into the boiling, choking midnight smoke I could see no one else, but after a while something white came out of the darkness toward me. It was a young girl, wearing what I took to be a nightgown—the lightest garment, at any event, she could have worn in this intolerable heat.

"What will happen to us?" she said, as soon as she saw me. "What will happen to us? Will it be the same tomorrow?"

"I don't know," I said. "What's your name?"

"Margaret." She coughed. "This must be the end of the world. If the sun is like this tomorrow—"

"It *is* the end of the world," I said. "But maybe it's the beginning of another. You and I will live to see it."

"How do you know?"

"By your name. The voices call you the mother of the new gods. Have you heard the voices?"

She moved away from me a little bit. There was a sudden, furious gust of wind, and a long line of sparks flew through the lurid sky overhead. "The voices?" she said.

"Yes. The voices of the powers which have done all this. They have promised to save us, you and I. Together we can recreate—"

Suddenly, she was running. She vanished almost instantly into darkness and the smoke. I ran after her, calling, but it was hopeless. Besides, my throat was already raw, and in the heat and the aftermath of the day I had no strength. I went back to my crypt. Tomorrow would tell the tale.

Sleep was impossible. I waited for dawn, and watched for it through my periscope from the buried vault of the bank where, a day before, I had been a kind of teller. This had been no ordinary bank, and I had never taken or issued any money; but otherwise the terms are just. Perhaps you have already guessed, for no ordinary vault is equipped with periscopes to watch the surrounding countryside. This was Fort Knox, a bed of gold to be seeded with promise of the Age of Gold under this golden fire.

And at last the sun came up. It was immense. But I waited a while, and watched the image of it which was cast from the periscope eyepiece onto the opposite wall of the vault. It was not as big as it had been yesterday. And where yesterday the direct rays from the periscope had instantly charred a thousand-dollar bill, today they made only a slowly growing brown spot which never found its kindling point.

The lesson was plain. Today most of what remained of mankind would be slain. But there would be survivors.

Then I slept.

I awoke toward the end of the day and set about the quest which I knew I must make. I took nothing with me but water, which I knew I could not expect to find. Then I left the vault forever.

The world which greeted me as I came to the surface was a world transformed, blasted. Nearly everything had been leveled, and the rest lay in jumbled, smoking ruins. The sky was completely black. Near the western horizon the swollen sunk sank, still monstrous, but now no hotter than the normal sun at the height of a tropic day. The great explosion, whatever it had been, was nearly over.

And now I had to find Margaret, and fulfill the millennium which the voices had promised. The tree of man had been blasted, but still it bore one flower. It was my great destiny to bring that flower to fruit.

Thus I bring this record to a close. I leave it here in the vault. Then I shall go forth into the desert of the world. If any find it, remember: I am your father and the father of your race. If not, you will all be smoke.

Now I go. My knife is in my hand.

My name is Andy Virchow, but probably you know me better as Admiral Universe. Nowhere in the pages of galactic history has there ever been a greater champion of justice. Who do you know that doesn't know Universe, ruler of the spaceways, hero of science, bringer of law and order in the age of the conquest of space? Not a planetary soul, that's who.

Of course not everybody knows that Andy Virchow is Admiral Universe. Sometimes I have to go in disguise and fool criminals. Then I am Andy Virchow, and they think I am only eight years old, until I have them where I want them and I whip out my Cosmic Smoke Gun and reveal my identification.

Sometimes I don't say who I am but just clean the crooks up and ride off in my rocket, the *Margy II*. Then afterwards the people I have saved say, "He didn't even stay to be thanked. I wonder who he was?" and somebody else says, "There's only one man on the frontiers of space like him. That's Admiral Universe."

My rocket is called the *Margy II* partly because my secret interstellar base is on Mars and the Mars people we call Martians call themselves Margies and I like to think of myself as a Margy *too*, because the people of Earth don't understand me and I do good for them because I am champion of justice, not because I like them. Then they're sorry, but it's too late. Me and the Margies understand each other. They ask me for advice before they do anything important, and I tell them what to do. Earth people are always trying to tell other people what to do. The Margies aren't like that, they ask what to do instead of always giving orders.

Also Admiral Universe calls his rocket *Margy II*, because my patron saint is St. Margaret who gets me out of trouble if I do anything wrong. Admiral Universe never does anything wrong because St. Margaret is on his side all the time. St. Margaret is the patron saint of clocks and is called the Mother of Galaxies, because she was a mother—not like my mother, who is always shouting and sending me to bed too early—and mothers have milk and *galaxy* is Greek for milk. If you didn't know I was Admiral Universe you'd ask how I know what's Greek for anything, but Admiral Universe is a great scientist and knows everything. Besides, my father was a teacher of Greek before he died and he was Admiral Universe's first teacher.

In all the other worlds in the universe everything is pretty perfect except for a few crooks that have to be shot. It's not like Earth at all. The planets are different from each other, but they are all happy and have lots of science and the people are kind and never raise their hands to each other or send each other to bed without their supper.

Sometimes there are terrible accidents in the spacelanes and Admiral Universe arrives on the scene in the nick of time and saves everybody, and all the men shake his hand and all the girls kiss him and say mushy things to him, but he refuses their thanks in a polite way and disappears into the trackless wastes of outer space because he carries a medal of St. Margaret's in his pocket over his heart. She is his only girl, but she can't ever be anybody's girl because she is a saint, and this is Admiral Universe's great tragedy which he never tells anybody because it's his private business that he has to suffer all by himself, and besides if anybody else knew it they would think he was mushy too and wouldn't be so afraid of him, like crooks I mean.

Admiral Universe is always being called from all over outer space to help people and sometimes he can't be one place because he has to be in some other place. Then he has to set his jaw and do the best he can and be tough about the people he can't help because he is helping somebody else. First he asks St. Margaret what he should do and she tells him. Then he goes and does it, and he is very sorry for the people who got left out, but he knows that he did what was right.

This is why I wasn't there when the sun blew up, because I was helping people somewhere else at the time. I didn't even know it was the sun, because I was so far away that it was just another star, and I didn't see it blow up, because stars blow up all the time and if you're Admiral Universe you get used to it and hardly notice. Margaret might have told me, but she's a saint, and doesn't care.

If I'd been there I would have helped. I would have saved my friends, and all the great scientists, and the girls who might be somebody's mothers some day, and everybody that was anybody except Dr. Ferguson, I would have left him behind to show him how wrong he was about me.

But I wasn't there at the time, and besides Admiral Universe never did like the Earth much. Nobody will really miss it.

My name is T. V. Andros. My father was an Athenian immigrant and a drunkard. After he came here he worked in the mines, but not very often because he was mostly soused.

Sometimes he beat my mother. She had TB but she took good care of us until I was eight; early that year my father got killed in a brawl in a bar, and the doctor—his name I forget—sent her back to the little town in Pennsylvania where she was born. She died that March.

After that I worked in the mines. The law says a kid can't work in the mines but in company towns the law don't mean much. I got the cough too but the other miners took care of me and I grew up tough and could handle myself all right.

When I was fourteen, I killed a man with a pick-handle, one blow. I don't remember what we were fighting about.

Mostly I kept out of fights, though. I had a crazy idea I wanted to educate myself and I read a lot—all kinds of things. For a while I read those magazines that tell about going to other planets and stuff like that. I didn't learn anything, except that to learn good you need a teacher, and the last one of those had been run out by the company cops. They said he was a Red.

It was tough in the mines. It's dark down there and hot, and you can't breathe sometimes for the dust. And you can't never wash the dirt off, it gets right down into your skin and makes you feel black even at noon on Sundays when you've scrubbed till your skin's raw.

I had a sixteen-year-old girl but I was too dirty for her. I tried to go to the priest about it but he wasn't looking for nothing but sin, and kept asking me had I done anything wrong with the girl. When I said I hadn't he wasn't interested no more. I hadn't, either, but he made me so mad he made me wish I had. After that I sort of drifted away from going to church because I couldn't stand his face. Maybe that was bad but it had its good side, too; I missed it and I took to cracking the Bible now and then. I never got much of the Bible when I was going to church.

After a while, I took to drinking something now and then. It wasn't right for a kid but I wasn't a kid no more, I was eighteen and besides in a company town there ain't nothing else to do. It helped some but not enough. All the guys in the bar ever talk about are wages and women. You got to drink yourself blind and stupid to keep from hearing them, otherwise you go nuts. After a while I was blind and stupid a lot of the time and didn't no longer know what I did or didn't.

Once when I was drunk I mauled a girl younger than I was; I don't know why I did it. She was just the age I had been when my mother left me to go home and die. Then it was all up with me at the mines. I didn't mean her any harm but the judge gave me the works. Two years.

I got clean for once in my life while I was in the jug and I did some more reading but it just mixed me up more. Two years is a long time. When I got out I felt funny in my head. I couldn't stop thinking about the girl who thought I was too dirty for her. I was at the age when I needed girls.

But I wasn't going to mess with girls my age who could see the prison whiteness on the outside and all that ground-in coal dust underneath it. I couldn't forget Maggy, the girl that got me into the jam. That had been a hot night in summer, with a moon as big as the sun, as red as blood. I hadn't meant her any harm. She reminded me of myself when my mother had gone away.

I found another Maggy and when the cops caught me they worked me over. I can't hear in one ear now and my nose is skewed funny on my face. I had it coming because I hurt the girl. When they let me out again I got a job as a super, but there was another girl in the apartment above, and I went to fix a pipe there while her mother was away. It was a hot day with a big sun and no air moving, just like the day my mother left. I didn't really know nothing had happened until I saw that one of my hands was dark red. Then I tried to get her to talk to me but she wouldn't move. After a while I felt some woman's hands beating at my neck. She said, "Stop, you!"

This time they took me to a hospital and a Dr. Ferdinand talked to me. Write it all down, he said. It may help you. So I wrote it all down, like you see it here. Then they put me in a cell and said I would have to stay for a while. I don't talk to them much any more.

It is a real hot day. Outside the cell the sun is bigger. I don't breathe good any more but there's something wrong with the air. I pulled my mattress to pieces but I didn't find nothing.

Maybe something is going to happen. Something is going to happen.

My name is Man. I will write my story if you wish.
I was . . .
Here the ashes blow away. The voices die.